DEADLY
BLISS

A CREE BLUE PSYCHIC EYE MYSTERY BOOK 5

Kate Allenton

Published by Coastal Escape
Publishing

Discover other titles by Kate Allenton
At

http://www.kateallenton.com

ISBN- 978-1-944237-48-6

DEADLY BLISS

Chapter 1

I stared at my reflection in the mirror and let my gaze flow down the last dress I'd wear as a single woman. My wealth of hair was styled to perfection. Not one flaw on display. I was the picture of perfect. I smiled. My heart, hopes, and dreams were finally aligned. The silky wedding dress was everything I'd ever dreamed of, even better than the one I'd envisioned as a little girl covered in rainbow-colored pixie dust with embedded neon lights. West might not have married me if I'd sauntered down the aisle in that. Who was I kidding? He would have loved anything I wore. He'd embraced my crazy long ago.

My bouquet was filled with roses from my Grammy's garden. I could almost imagine her spirit popping in any minute complaining that I'd stolen a few. I couldn't have asked for anything more perfect. I'd come a long way from the lonely person I used to be who sent anonymous psychic predictions through the mail.

Apprehension and excitement filled my veins. In less than thirty minutes I'd be his wife. Mrs. Archer. I wrinkled my nose. "Mrs. Blue- Archer."

"Sounds like a superhero." Roni leaned in to inspect her reflection in the full-length mirror, running her finger over her front teeth to wipe away the lipstick residue.

"I think it sounds perfect," Charlotte handed me the bouquet. My best friend always knew exactly what to say, even though at times I was stubborn and a pain in her rear. She was good at putting me in my place.

Mrs. Simmons, the wedding planner, peeked her head inside. "It's time, ladies. Everyone is in position."

Excitement skirted my spine. A squeal escaped my lips. "It's time."

I wasn't much of a squealer, but today was different. I was marrying the most perfect man. Who would have thought he'd be a reformed killer super-secret agent ex-spy?

"Any unwanted guests of the murdered ghostly kind?" Charlotte whispered to Roni as they followed me out the door.

"Bite your tongue," I said, glancing back. "Don't tempt fate. She doesn't like me."

Mrs. Simmons held a trained eye on her watch as we entered the hall. She was in charge of keeping our schedule, and she was as efficient as a double shot of espresso. I didn't care about the time. Today had felt like the longest day of the year to me. This moment couldn't get here fast enough.

Retired Police Officer John Faraday had been there for me since the day I was born. Freddie, well he was another story, a reformed mobster who decided I was useless at protecting myself. Turns out he was right. Then there's the Prince of Wellington. The royal who doesn't know what the word monogamy means. They were all waiting impatiently in the hallway outside the closed double doors. If it had been up to me, we would have sent the Prince of Secrets and Lies a postcard after our honeymoon. His presence was the only concession I'd made. It was his screw-ups, though, that had sent West directly into my path. It wouldn't be right to tell him to kiss my ass. Well, I could, but it might not end well for him. Okay, so maybe I still held a grudge against everything that had gone down in California because of Prince Cheats-a-lot. But heck, West and I almost died because of the royal family.

Yet, there he stood, waiting like any best man should.

"You look lovely," the prince said, kissing my cheek.

I bit back my string of inappropriate replies and smiled. "Thank you."

He held out his arm for Charlotte to take. Better her than my newfound young cousin, Roni. In my mind, she was still jailbait, although she'd already turned eighteen three weeks ago. A miracle I hadn't been expecting happened that day.

She'd decided to stay. Her reason; family had to stick together. Seemed our generation was the only one that appreciated that sentiment.

I shoved those thoughts aside as Mrs. Simmons opened the door, sending Prince of Hell and Charlotte down the aisle. Two beats later, she sent out Roni and Freddie. When the door closed, I held Faraday's gaze. He was one of the few that knew the Blues' secrets. Uncontrollable laughter spilled from my lips. I was really doing this.

"I'm sorry," I said, trying to stifle my laugh.

"I wouldn't expect anything else." Faraday's face softened as he held out his arm. "Your parents would have been so proud of you."

"Really? Because I've screwed up a bunch, and I can say with almost 100% certainty that it's going to happen again."

"I'm sure they're pleased as spiked punch." He jostled his head toward the exit. "There's still time to change your mind. I can hold them off at the door if you want to make a run for it."

"I thought you approved of West."

He shrugged. "He seems to love you, and I know he can keep you safe. I just thought maybe you'd end up with a cop."

I rolled my eyes. "Cop? Please... I prefer the renegade spy smooth-talking type. I'm not changing my mind."

He pulled a travel-size bottle of whiskey from his pocket and took a sip, offering the same to me.

Liquor wouldn't help drown the butterflies dancing in my belly. I declined in favor of savoring every moment.

He snapped his fingers at Mrs. Simmons, earning him a stern look of disapproval. "Okay, lady, you're up."

That was Faraday. He never missed a beat when it came to pushing buttons.

Mrs. Simmons pushed the receiver in her ear. "It's a go. Start the march."

She pulled open the doors to the familiar tune I never thought would matter much to me. I smiled and squeezed Faraday's arm, leaning in to whisper, "They're here."

"The whole town is," he whispered back. "It's not every day they get a free ticket to watch your circus."

True as that was, they didn't matter half as much as the people he couldn't see. "Not them." My eyes started to tear.

"My mom, dad, and Grammy. They all came."

"Well, of course they did."

****

The wedding reception was dwindling down. The lights above were dim, the music slow as I swayed in West's arms.

"Mrs. Archer," he whispered in my ear.

"Mr. Blue," I whispered back.

His chest jostled as he chuckled. He stopped our sway to stare into my eyes. "I love you, Cree."

"I would hope so. You just promised to love me when I'm sick, and that's about as pretty as Faraday's wrinkled butt."

"Nice visual."

I winked and stood on my tiptoes until my mouth was inches from his. "I love you, back."

He pressed his lips to mine in a kiss that made my toes curl. This was my new life. He was my forever man. It wasn't until that moment that I realized everything that had happened up till this point brought me to him; to us. I couldn't imagine it working out any other way.

The room was divided like night and day. Faraday was shooting the breeze in easy banter with the police chief and fellow police officers on one side of the room. They had a lot of catching up to do.

On the other side of the room, Mob boss, Moreno, and his nephew were sitting with Roni, Charlotte, and Freddie.

There was an unspoken truce between the law-abiding and breakers. I'd wanted them both to attend. West and I lived in the gray area, where the colors blurred.

"You're thinking too much," West whispered as the song slowly faded away.

"That's what happens when you pick a wife with a brain." I took his hand and led him to our table. Settling into our seats, we toasted with champagne. I could get drunk simply from the heat and love in his tender gaze. I'd hit the jackpot with this one. No more fishes in the sea for me.

The reception room doors opened, pulling my gaze. The baker entered, a look of irritation lining his face. He spotted Roni across the room. She'd been the one I'd tasked with handling any problems with the dessert. He headed for her with a laser focus, his strides determined until he reached her table. I couldn't hear his voice, although his hands flailed like he was swatting at monster-sized mosquitoes in a swamp.

This couldn't be good. I slowly started to rise from my seat, embracing my impulsive behavior to fix whatever was wrong.

"She's got this," he rested his hand on my arm.

It wasn't Roni I was worried about. She was 100% certifiably all Blue. I slowly lowered, reclaiming my seat.

Roni slammed her knife into the table. The handle standing upright as it stuck into the hard surface. The baker took a shocked step back. This wasn't going to end well for one of them. I started to rise again when West cupped my hand. "Trust her."

Roni whispered something into Charlotte's ear. She flexed her balled fist, shaking out the anger in her palms as she followed the baker out.

"See. She's already calming down."

"I should go..." My words died watching Charlotte's hurried approach, the blood drained from her face, palms up in a gesture to stay calm. Her gesture did the opposite.

"Can I worry now?" I asked West.

"Only if you want me to worry too, luv."

"They had a problem with the cake," Charlotte announced.

"What kind of problem?" I asked, finally standing.

Charlotte bit her lip in the way she only ever did when she was debating what to say. "The cake had an accident, but Roni went to take care of it."

"What kind of accident? Like strawberry instead of chocolate or layers smashed into the dirt?" I asked, squeezing West's hand.

"The baker wouldn't say."

This was worse than bad. My gaze flew to the knife standing erect on the table. Roni probably had another one tucked away and was threatening them with their lives if it didn't get fixed.

"Go." West kissed my cheek. "Stop her before she kills one of them."

"Aw, hun. You really do know me." I kissed him back.

Before I took the first step, the reception doors flew open, and four men entered. Two in uniform headed toward the chief and Faraday's table. The other two I recognized as Moreno's guys, headed in their boss's direction.

I clenched West's hands tighter as I watched the deputies whisper in the chief's ear. My gaze flew to Moreno as his guys did the same. "This isn't good."

When the royal guards who had been stationed outside hurried to the prince's side, I knew all hell was about to break loose.

"Okay, now we can worry," West answered.

The chief and Faraday rose from their seats. Moreno and Freddie did the same.

Silence blanketed the room as everyone curiously watched both parties headed for the door. Even the music had vanished.

"I'll be right back." West left my side for Prince-Cry-Baby and spoke in hushed tones.

Charlotte and I stood helplessly by. Whoever was ruining my beautiful day was about to get a double dose of Blue.

"Someone needs to tell me what the hell is going on." My voice came out on the verge of hysterics.

West dropped his head in a silent shake before pulling his gun from beneath his tux. Damn it to all hell. This was real. Not just a bad dream. West never pulled his gun unless he planned to use it.

"Damn it, I left my guns in my other dress." I kicked off my heels and lifted my dress and started jogging in West's direction as he headed for the door. We pulled the doors open and were greeted by two police officers stepping in our way.

"Everyone just stay calm."

"What happened?" I demanded.

West answered. "All kitchen staff was tied up and left in the freezer. No sign of Roni."

My brows dipped in confusion. "Who took her?"

"They don't know yet," a guard offered. "We have orders to keep everyone inside the reception hall. I'm sorry, Mrs. Archer."

"Mrs. Blue-Archer," West corrected.

"Your wedding is officially a hostage situation."

Chapter 2

"Who the hell took her?" I growled, wishing like hell I'd brought a gun to threaten them with.

The officers exchanged a hesitant look. "The chief will be in to make an announcement. I suggest you two resume your party before you send everyone into a state of panic."

"Panic?" I asked, and my brows shot up as I hit West's arm. "I need your phone."

He handed it to me, and I turned my back on the guards, punching in Roni's number.

It was answered on the third ring.

"Roni, oh thank God," I said as relief swarmed through my body. "Where are you?"

"I'm afraid Roni can't come to the phone at the moment. She's a little tied up," a male voice answered.

I spun around to West as I struggled to breath.

"Who is this?" I asked.

"My name is of no concern, but I can assure you, your cousin is alive."

"What do you want?"

"I'm in need of your assistance."

"Why would I help you?"

"If you'd like to see Roni again, I need you to listen closely. In five minutes the fire alarm is going to sound and create mass panic. Everyone but you is going to be heading toward the guards at the door. "

I held West's gaze as the psychopath continued speaking.

"You are to remain in the middle of the dance floor, alone. Do you understand?"

"Now I know you're crazy if you think I'll go anywhere with you willingly."

"There are explosives in the building and attached to three different cars in the parking area. If you don't want to be responsible for deaths, you'll do as you're told."

"See, now there's the thing," I said, resting my fist on my waist. "You must not know me if you think I'd be compliant."

"Is that so?" he asked.

A second later an explosion sounded from the parking lot, and my party guests started to panic. West grabbed my arm and ushered me across the room, his gun resting in his hand.

"I can assure you that I'm serious, Mrs. Archer."

"What do you want?" My voice rose in anger with each syllable.

"I want you in the middle of the dance floor when the alarms sound. Leave your husband behind, or he dies. Don't do as I ask and Roni dies. Tell the police, and I blow the building. Am I clear?"

"Clear as muddy water, you jackass," I growled.

"I was warned you were a feisty one."

"I can't wait to show you up close and personal."

"You now have four minutes to convince your husband not to follow you."

I snapped the phone closed and held West's gaze. "I need your gun."

"What is going on?"

I shrugged and popped the clip to make sure it was loaded. "A madman has Roni, and if I don't do what he says, then he's going to blow the building."

"You aren't going anywhere without me."

I lifted my foot onto the chair and pulled my dress up to shove the gun in my garter belt. "If you follow me, he'll kill everyone. There are bombs set up around the building and on three cars in the lot. If you follow me, he'll blow them."

"Not if I kill him first," West answered, pulling another gun out of a leg holster.

"Please, I can't lose her."

"I can't lose you."

I tapped the face of my watch. The same watch that West and Freddie had put a tracker in. "You won't. If I don't call you at the top of every hour, call in the FBI or, better yet, Moreno's guys. They don't have a problem with shooting first and asking questions later."

"Cree. Don't do this. Let me go."

I pressed my finger to his lips silencing him before placing a hard, heated kiss on his mouth. "I love you. If I call you and I'm in trouble, I'll say the word cake."

"Please, luv. You don't know what you're walking into."

"He has Roni," I said. "When they release everyone, trace her phone, but keep your distance until I have her."

West grabbed my hand and pulled me to the prince's table where one his guards remained. "Give me your earpiece."

The man's brows dipped. "No."

"Do it, or I'll kill you."

The man pulled the earpiece out and gently wiped it off handing it to West. West held it up in front of my eyes. "I'm going to be the little birdie in your ear." He gentle nudged the plastic inside my ear and moved my hair to cover it from view.

"I'll find you." West kissed me long and hard before letting me walk to the middle of the dance floor, and I held West's gaze just as the fire alarm sounded.

"I'm counting on it."

DEADLY BLISS

Chapter 3

Everything happened in a flash. Chaos reigned as all of the party guests rushed the door, pushed the officers out of the way. Everyone except West and me. He stood where I'd left him, his gaze on mine, when in a swish, like a magician's trap door, the floor vanished beneath my feet.

A scream left my lips until I landed with a thud on a mattress of some sort beneath my back. I struggled to sit as West stared at me from above.

"I'm okay," I answered, blinking rapidly to adjust my eyes to the creepy darkness. The sound of a phone ringing had me scanning the area. A table sat nearby. Whoever I was dealing with must have done some serious planning. I grabbed it and answered.

"Hello."

"Very good, Mrs. Blue."

"Archer," I corrected. "Only my friends call me Blue."

"There is a flashlight on the table. Take it and turn to the hallway behind you. In ten klicks you'll emerge, and we will pick you up."

"Ten klicks?" I said, loud enough for West to hear and pointed in the direction of the hallway. "I'm afraid you'll have to elaborate in southern terms. Is that like find the Tin Man and follow the yellow brick road or more like turn at the second swamp?"

"Go to the end of the tunnel, Mrs. Blue."

"Archer," I growled. "End of the creepy tunnel it is," I said louder and grabbed the flashlight. Flicking it on, I headed into the darkness.

I strained to hear everything as I flicked the light around the dirty unused tunnel. I was dragging the train of my dress over decades-old dirt and grime. This man was going to die a slow painful death for ruining my special day.

The thick, musty air choked me as I advanced cautiously with calculated steps. Rocks from the tunnel pained my feet, but even that wouldn't stop me from finding Roni. That girl...I sighed.

Each breath was loud in my ears as I weaved around a corner. Moonlight shown at the end of the tunnel. A soft breeze caressed my face as I tried climbing out of the hole. Dirt covered the front of my fifty-pound dress as I struggled to pull myself out.

Hands grabbed my arms from both sides and lifted me out with ease.

"Mrs. Archer," one of the men said as I was placed on my feet.

"Bad people," I answered in greeting.

"If you'll come with us, please." One of the guys pointed his machine gun toward a waiting SUV.

"Polite bad people. That's new."

One of the guys held the door open for me as I struggled to climb inside. Another one behind me grabbed the bottom of my dress and shoved it inside, filling half the space.

There was nothing in the SUV that told me who these wedding-crasher terrorists might be. I waited until the polite one climbed in on the other side of the SUV and machine gun guy slid behind the wheel.

"Who are you guys?"

They didn't answer. Hired hit men? Maybe, but it had been awhile since I'd pissed anyone off.

"The silent type," I said and glanced out the window as the SUV began to move. "Your wives must have trained you well." I opened the energies around me to see if I could get a read on any of these guys. It had been a long time since I'd used that particular ability. I glanced at the guy next to me. "Congrats."

His brows dipped even though he kept his eyes trained ahead.

"You must have a lot of determination to quit smoking."

He turned to me, and I shrugged. "You should put some ice on your knee. It's twisted, right?"

He didn't answer, but the driver did. "Shut up."

"Mystery Voice never told me I needed to be quiet, just not create a fuss. I haven't broken any rules."

He glanced in the rearview mirror, meeting the other bad guy's gaze. I leaned forward, opening my energies to the driver's. He was going to be much more fun to play with. "You need to fix that slow leak in your basement. It's not from the roof. It's your water heater. I'd hate for you to choke on the mold growing in your walls."

"I said shut up," he growled.

"No...I don't think I will." I turned my gaze to the window again. "Your boss needs me alive. He actually said he needs my help. He tipped his hand."

"Who the hell are you?" the man sitting next to me asked.

"One pissed-off bride." They didn't know it yet, but when this was over, I was going to hex their asses or at least give them a lifelong case of heartburn with the added bonus of acid reflux. I knew someone in the French quarter who could do that and more. I'd be on them like the stench of skunk spray in the hot afternoon sun.

We traveled down country back roads, stopping at a barbwire fence protected by more men dressed in black suits carrying guns like the two that had me. I leaned forward and rested my arms on the seat back. "If I didn't know better, I'd say the Weston Plantation was aiding and abetting terrorists."

Our SUV was ushered through the gate, and we came to a stop in front of the mansion. It looked like someone had transplanted the white house onto farmlands. What a waste. This pretty house wouldn't be left standing after West arrived.

The polite guy got out and rounded the car, helping me out. "We aren't terrorists."

"No?" I glanced at his gun. "Just well-armed kidnappers who are willing to hurt people. I'm sure your momma would be proud."

"She's dead." All expression vacated his face while he guided me by the arm. Seems I had a knack for making new friends.

"I'm sure my dead Grammy will be glad to track her down and pass the message."

He pulled me to a stop while the driver terrorist yanked the front door open. "You better hope you're as good as he thinks you are."

"You should be worried he's right." I walked into the mansion, my gaze going to my surrounding, not in the way of admiring it but to find what I could break and use as a weapon.

"Honey, I'm home." My voice echoed from the vaulted ceilings like a tourist visiting the Grand Canyon. Sonar and radar might come in handy. Too bad I wasn't a superhero.

The beefy fingers around my arm dug into my skin as I was yanked again to keep walking. The polite kidnapper shoved open a pair of double doors while beefy fingers guided me inside.

A man sat at a rectangular ornate cherry table. As if that wasn't cliché enough, he was using the fine china. Finally, I could put a face with the voice running these militant thugs.

His hair was as dark as the anger bubbling in my soul. His designer suit looked as though it cost more than my now dirty wedding dress. The watch on his arm even more so. I opened up my abilities to see what this guy was up to. The first thing that popped into my head was a name. Not sure if it was his, but it looked like it might fit him.

"Malcolm Nunnery," I said before I could stop myself and use the element of surprise.

"I'm impressed." His smile disappeared behind his cloth napkin while he wiped his face. He rose from his seat and gestured to the opposite end of the table. "Please have a seat."

"Where is Roni?"

"She's fine," he answered, and goosebumps covered my arms. He was telling the truth.

"What do you want?" I yanked my arm from the terrorist hit man's hold and crossed my arms over my chest.

"For you to sit," he answered.

I glanced at my watch as I moved to take a seat.

His brows dipped as he glanced at his own expensive watch. This guy was observant. Seven thirty. I had exactly thirty more minutes before all hell was about to rain down on this place if I didn't make my call. Charlotte, West, the chief and probably even the FBI had been called in by now.

The beeping light of my tracker was probably driving West nuts by now. If I had to guess he was already parked somewhere nearby trying to figure out the best way to get in undetected. I loved that man.

Nunnery glanced to the polite terrorist that had quit smoking and jerked his head toward the door. "Alert the others to expect company and arrange transport. We'll be leaving soon."

I grinned and sat back in my chair. "Mind reader?"

"Hardly. Since I underestimated you and our time is limited, how about we cut to the chase. I need your help."

"And now why would I help a terrorist who kidnapped me from my own wedding?"

"Friendship," he answered smugly.

"We aren't friends." I raised my brow in challenge.

"I'm an acquired taste, but it wasn't my friendship that I was referring to."

"Well, all my friends are accounted for. So...." I rested my hand over the knife in front of me.

"Not all." He snapped his fingers. A door across the room opened, and Glynis, the daughter of the deputy director of the FBI, walked into the room. She was pale, her movements weak. Her legs looked as though they were ready to give out. Nunnery was out of his seat and took Glynis by the arm, gently guiding her to the table.

"I'm sorry, Cree. I told them I didn't want you involved."

I got out of my chair and squatted by her side. "What happened?"

Glynis' eyes were unfocused, and her breathing shallow as Nunnery took smelling salts from his pocket and held the packet under her nose.

Her eyes opened wide, and he proceeded to hold a glass of water to her lips.

"She's been drugged," he answered.

"What the hell did you give her?" I growled.

Chapter 4

"It wasn't him, Cree. Malcolm is trying to help me," Glynis answered.

Nunnery helped lift Glynis from her seat, whisked her off her feet, and carried her out of the room. Moments later he returned, just long enough for me to slip the gun from my garter and rest it on my lap.

"I knew you wouldn't believe me unless she told you herself."

"What's wrong with her?"

"She was poisoned. The antidote that can cure her is being held for ransom."

"By whom?"

"Best guess?" Deputy Director Harrison Reed said, escorting Roni into the room with him. "Terrorists."

Roni raised her brow. "Some friends you've got here, Cree."

"You'll have to forgive us. Time isn't on our side," Harrison said, standing next to the table. I rose with West's gun in my hand. Nunnery's eyes widened in alarm.

"Two more minutes and I would have shot your balls off."

"I warned you she was feisty." Harrison chuckled. "No need for the gun. You can put that back where you got it from."

I lifted my leg up onto a chair and fumbled through the crinoline until I found my garter belt and shoved it back into its hiding spot.

Harrison dropped a file on the table. "We've been trying to track this guy for a week with no luck."

I flipped the file open to a fuzzy picture of a man in a hoodie hiding his face. "What does he want in return for giving you the antidote?"

"You," Harrison answered.

My gaze snapped to his. "Why me? I'm a nobody."

"He hasn't elaborated why, only that he won't speak to anyone but you. Please, just talk to him and find out what he's after," Harrison begged.

I slowly nodded. Talking I could do. Not pissing the guy off, that might be hard. "Why the theatrics? Why not just ask me? You know I would have helped."

"It's a matter of national security, and we couldn't risk losing time if the local cops stepped in," Nunnery answered, earning my glare. "She isn't the only one sick."

"Just who the hell are you?" I asked.

"Malcolm Nunnery, Director of the Secret Service."

My brows dipped as I slowly started to realize the implications of the FBI and Secret Service in the same room. "Which one? The president or his son?"

"Both."

Holy mother of God. I held out my hand to Harrison. "I need your phone."

"You can't tell anyone," he answered.

I jerked my hand in a give-it-to-me now response. "You need to trust me, or there are going to be even more casualties."

He handed me the phone before sharing a look with Nunnery. I quickly dialed West's number, and he answered on the first ring. "Hello."

"Hey, hun. You need to stand down. I don't need a rescue."

"What the hell is going on?"

"A friend needs my help, so call off the extraction and tell Moreno and his guys not to engage."

"Mobster Moreno?" Nunnery asked Reed.

I covered the receiver. "He's a friend, and he doesn't like it when his friends are kidnapped. You would have done the same thing...hell, you did." I answered before returning my attention to my husband. "I'm fine, honey. I promise."

"How do I know they aren't coercing you into telling me that?"

"Here, I'll let you hear a familiar voice." I held the phone up to Harrison. "Tell him hello."

"Uh...hello," Harrison said.

I pointed the phone to Roni. "You too."

"She's fine," Roni said. "We're all fine. It's just one big freaking heyday. She's already put the gun away, and I haven't had to cut anyone. Tell Damien I'll call him later."

I shoved the phone to my ear and tried for my best calm voice. "Believe me now?"

"What the hell does Harrison want you involved in?"

"Well, here's the thing," I said, holding Harrison's gaze.

He shook his head, and Nunnery pulled a gun, pointing it to my head at the same time Roni had one out pointing at his head.

Harrison reached for his empty holster and sighed. I'd have to get Roni to teach me her pick pocketing skills. Those might come in handy one day. "You want my help? He's involved. He's my husband."

Harrison nodded.

"You can come in now," I said, ending the call and handing it back to Harrison.

West walked into the room from where Glynis had been taken. He had his gun in his hand.

"What the..." Nunnery said, lowering his gun, and Roni lowered hers.

"She's my wife," West answered, closing the distance between us. He looked me over and spotted the bruise on my arm.

I covered it with my hand. "I'm okay, really."

"How did you know he was already here?" Nunnery asked.

"Because he's my husband," I said, pulling the earpiece out of my ear. I handed it to West before pressing a kiss to his lips. "You didn't kill anyone getting in here, did you?"

"No one even noticed," he answered. "Glynis wasn't looking too hot. Is she okay?"

"No," Harrison answered.

West had his phone out and started to text.

"What are you doing?"

"Calling off the calvary," West answered, sliding the phone back into his pocket. "Are we done here?"

I slid my arm through West's and laid my head on his shoulder. He was such a good husband walking into eminent danger. We were going to have to talk about that. "They need me to negotiate with someone holding the antidote to fix Glynis."

West's smile fell into a frown. "Why you?"

I didn't answer.

"Why her?" he asked Harrison.

"The ransom caller requested her."

"Whose phone is she supposed to use?" West sometimes asked the oddest questions, but I loved him anyway.

"Mine," Harrison answered.

West pulled his phone out again, and this time placed a call. "Charlotte, I need you to call all of your connections and ask the others to hack Deputy Director Reed's phone and trace the call that he's about to make. Text me when you're a go."

"We've tried that," Nunnery answered. "We couldn't get a lock on his location."

West smiled. "Humor me."

"Charlotte's good, but she isn't that good," Harrison said.

Ye of little faith. My best friend was the best. "She's made some new friends now that she's with Freddie. I think a few might be on your watch list."

"Oh no," Nunnery said, balling his fists and resting them on his waist. "No one else can know."

"Relax, they're hackers, and they'll help find the location. That is what we all want, isn't it? To catch this guy and skin him alive."

Minutes later West's phone chirped, and he pulled it from his pocket. "They're ready whenever you are."

"That was quick." Harrison's brows dipped. "We'll be talking about these new friendships when everything is over."

Apprehension crossed Harrison's face as he handed me his phone. A look of worry like I'd never seen filled his eyes. His world hinged on me finding the answers. Talk about pressure. I held the phone to my chest. "How do you know this guy even has an antidote?"

Harrison pulled a small vial from his pocket. "He gave me enough to keep each of them alive for two weeks. We have scientists trying to back into the formula, but it could take months."

"Explains why she didn't show up at the wedding."

"She wanted to." Harrison's sad gaze held mine. "She really did."

My gaze dropped to the vial in his hand. "I'm going to need that vial and his note."

"Why?" Nunnery asked.

"My backup plan," I answered.

Chapter 5

We sat down around the table, and I dialed the number Harrison gave me. I grabbed a roll from the basket and tore off a piece and shoved it in my mouth. Nunnery's gaze dipped, and I shrugged. "What? You kidnapped me. The least you can do is feed me. I'm hungry."

"I'll buy you steaks for the rest of your life if you get the antidote."

I grinned. "I'll hold you to that, but instead of steak, make it Jamaican Blue Mountain coffee; lots of it."

"About time," the machine-over voice said. I hated altered voices. They were so impersonal.

"That's my fault," I said, shoving another piece of roll in my mouth. "I wasn't a willing participant until I knew what was at stake." Steak, nice, big, and juicy, mouthwatering; that was going to be my meal of choice at the reception.

"Ms. Blue?" he asked.

"I haven't decided yet. It's a toss-up between Mrs. Blue, Mrs. Blue- Archer, or Mrs. Archer. They say when you get married to try and maintain your identity, but seeing how you know me as Blue, I think a change might be good for me."

"You're very nonchalant about this call with so much at stake, Cree."

"I was pulled from my freakin' wedding. If you wanted a professional, deal with the three letter agencies..."

"Smug even," he said.

I leaned in closer to the phone. "That's because I plan to track you down regardless of how this phone call goes. I'm warning you now. I will find you, and it won't be pretty."

The fake automated voice laughed. "It's not me you need to be concerned about finding."

"No? Well, I'll consider it a bonus. I don't like bullies. You've really screwed up now. Not only are you on the top of the FBI list, as well as all those three letter agencies, you're at the top of mine. That isn't a safe place to be with generations and generations of dead people at my disposal."

West had his phone out and was motioning for me to draw out the conversation.

"I'm counting on it," he answered. "Unfortunately for you, those three letter agencies didn't follow my instructions. They wasted a whole week trying to find me. That only leaves you seven days to find what I'm looking for or the world will be mourning with you."

"I'm not much of a crier. Sorry to disappoint. I'm more of a revenge seeker, so really it's you who should hope that I find whatever it is you're searching for. Because if she dies, you do too." I glanced at the others at the table. "And I'm sure all those three letter agencies will look the other way, if not provide the gun and bullets."

"If I'd wanted you dead, Cree, you would be. I'm sorry you're going to have to cancel your honeymoon in Cancun. That claw-footed bathtub in the honeymoon suite isn't as luxurious as you were hoping."

My gaze shot to West's. We'd just been discussing that bathtub in detail last night in bed. This fucker has been in my house.

"Game on, asshat. Tell me what you need me to find." I hoped to hell it was something I could blow up while he watched.

West glanced back down at his phone and scribbled down an address on a cloth napkin. He handed it to Nunnery, who hurried from the room.

"Not a what, Mrs. Blue. A who."

Even better.

"Who? Don't tell me it's your mommy. She doesn't want you to find her. She told me so."

"Now listen here—" The automated voice got deeper.

"No. You listen here, you sick fucking bastard. These aren't your rules; they're mine. You need me, not the other way around."

"Glynis might disagree," he said in a calmer tone.

"Glynis isn't going to care if I take the antidote from your cold dead hand. I might even keep one of your fingers as a souvenir. Now, as a show of good faith, I want you to give them the antidote, and I'll help you. Those are my terms."

"We aren't playing by your rules," he said, and I smirked as I shook my head and jabbed the phone, ending the call.

"What the hell did you just do?" Harrison jumped from his seat, and West did too. They were both arguing when the phone rang again.

Everyone stopped arguing and stared at the phone in disbelief. I couldn't believe it had actually worked. I mean, I'd seen it in a movie, but it had actually freakin' worked. I missed my calling as a negotiator. I answered on the third ring. "Hello..."

"Listen here—" His voice was even deeper with anger.

I smiled as I jabbed the button again. This was getting fun.

The room was silent after that. No more arguing. I think I'd stunned them all into silence, that is until the phone rang again.

I answered. "Lose the attitude, dude, because I give new meaning to the word hangry. You've ruined my wedding reception, you've bugged my house, and you hurt my friends. You've pissed off the wrong girl. Now show me a move of good faith, or this conversation is over. I'll never help, and the only person I'll be finding will be you. I promise that."

"The post office where you send your letters," he answered.

I lifted my gaze to Harrison. Only a handful of people knew where that was. I hadn't mailed a letter in a long while. This guy knew things about my past.

"Come alone. I'll leave one full vial and a list of instructions in a package in the mail bin."

"You going to leave me a key to get it open?" I asked.

"Now why would I need to do that? You already know how to pick that particular lock."

The line went dead.

Chapter 6

I slid the phone across the table to Harrison. "You have a mole. He's working with someone inside your agency."

Harrison ran his hand over his head. "I trust all of my men."

"Yeah? You sure about that?" I asked, standing from the table.

"With my life," the director answered.

It wasn't his life I was worried about. The director looked older now, tired, with more gray around the temples. "Well then, one has been compromised. You should vette them again."

"Will someone please explain what the hell is going on!" Roni exclaimed. "This is like Downton Abbey for freakin' spies."

It was worse than that if I was the only one who could help. I mean, seriously, these agencies had teams of people and secret projects testing psychics and crap. I'd seen a documentary just the other day. "I need to change my clothes. Breaking into a mail drop box in a wedding dress is going to garner me a few questionable stares."

"You don't have time to change," Nunnery argued, walking back into the room.

"Newsflash. This is my game now, and I'm the director of Blueville." I turned to West. "Would you be a dear and explain all of this to Roni and bring the car around?"

He kissed my cheek. "Your wish is my command, luv."

He was definitely a keeper. I turned back to Harrison with a raised brow. "Please make sure they don't shoot him and let him in the gate while I go visit with Glynis for a few minutes."

Harrison headed for the door with West and Roni following behind him. I grabbed my unfinished roll and slipped inside the room where Glynis had been carried.

The room was furnished like a bedroom with a hospital bed pressed against one wall. The dresser and table made out of solid, expensive wood. The only thing that differed was the added medical equipment. An IV drip was set up. A heart monitor was on the other side of the bed. It had the comforts of a bedroom with the perks of state-of-the-art medical equipment.

A nurse was napping in a nearby chair. The soft sound of her snores filled the room.

Glynis' gaze held mine as I approached. She looked so weak, not her usual vibrant, upbeat self. Seeing her like this was a travesty; a wrong that I was going to right. Someone was going to die a slow, painful death.

"I knew you were trouble when we met," I said, sitting down on the mattress beside her.

"I'm sorry I couldn't make it to the wedding." Her sad eyes held mine.

I shrugged. "You were a little under the weather. You're forgiven."

She coughed, her body jerking several times before she grabbed the oxygen mask and held it to her nose and took several long breaths.

"Any idea who this lunatic is?" I asked.

"I wish I knew."

"He's giving us a gesture of good faith by handing over one vial of the antidote."

"How did you manage that?" she asked, her eyes laced with concern.

"I used my charming personality."

Glynis started laughing, which threw her into another coughing fit. She grabbed the mask again.

My heart clenched, watching her. She wasn't supposed to die this way. I wasn't going to let her.

I rested my hand on hers. "Good news is there aren't any ghosts in the room to come welcome you over."

"Would you tell me if there were?"

I shook my head. "Bad news is that they're depending on me to play by this maniac's rules, and we both know I was never any good at following orders."

She removed her mask. "You don't have to do this."

"Yes, I do," I answered and rose from my spot. "What kind of friend would I be if I didn't save your life...twice?"

The first time had been by mere chance. An anonymous letter written to her dad about a man stalking her, intent on hurting her. She hadn't even noticed he'd targeted her as his next victim. Who knew the director of the FBI would take my warnings seriously. They'd caught the guy and pinned a bunch of serial killings on him, and he was scheduled to die soon. If he hadn't already.

DEADLY BLISS

Chapter 7

I sat in my Jeep in the parking garage I always used when I was playing *Mission Impossible*. A fast getaway was important when committing a crime. Night had fallen; my only accomplice was the moon hiding in a cloudy sky. I let out a shaky breath and felt for the gun strapped beneath my jacket and patted the two bobby pins in my hair. The perfect hiding place for law-breaking tools, not that I'd be arrested. Not tonight.

I slipped out of my car and snapped latex gloves over my hands in an attempt not to ruin whatever physical evidence Harrison and Nunnery could salvage. Attempted murder was going to be a hard charge to beat if this guy left DNA behind. Right now all they had was an address that might not pan out and a creepy automated voice to try to de-digitize. I'm sure one of the government organizations had super-secret gadgets that the public didn't know about. If not, I'd help them find an app for that. It could happen. Heck, they had one for communicating with ghosts.

I walked in sure strides, my gaze going back and forth over my surroundings. The post office was closed. The lights were off. No one nearby and only the lights in the parking garage and another building illuminated the area.

I stopped in front of the drop box and pulled the pins from my hair. Within seconds I eased the door open and spotted a package in the mail container. There were several, but only one had my name written in big black marker scrawled across the top. I shoved the other letters around it to the side.

I grabbed it and was about to shut the door when I spotted another letter sitting near it. The same funky R scribbled like in my name.

"Well, bite me." Apprehension sizzled down my spine as anger assaulted my very fiber. The letter was addressed to Edward Munz, in care of the state penitentiary, where the dirtbag was currently serving time for murder and stalking Glynis. Was this what it was all about? Had my dealings with the FBI came full circle?

I took the letter out of the bin and shoved it in my pocket. There was no such thing as coincidence. Not where I was concerned. I closed the mail drop box and jogged across the street with the package in hand.

I got that apprehensive feeling I normally got when my phone about to ring, so I slipped it out of my pocket along with the stolen letter. It was official; I was breaking the law.

My caller ID read Blocked Number as it rang, but I answered anyway.

"I see you got the package." A man spoke into the phone. Unlike the computerized voice that had given me instructions earlier, this one was a real living person. A voice I not only would remember but I'd testify against if he didn't end up dead first.

"You're watching me?" I glanced around the parking garage at all of the empty cars parked in the dark. Not a single human shadow stood out. He could have been watching and waiting from anywhere.

"I'm surprised you took the letter. You do know that you're breaking a federal law."

"Yeah, well, so are you," I said, tossing the package into my Jeep and scanning the other cars and dimly lit area for any movement. "Is that what this is about? You a friend of Munz's?"

"They are about to execute an innocent man," the anonymous caller said.

"The FBI caught him in his creepy lair and found all the proof of his kills. You're hard-pressed and a little messed up in the head if you think otherwise."

"Wrong person, right place. The FBI made a mistake... thanks to you."

"Listen, anonymous caller dude—"

"You can call me John."

"I'd rather call you a raving lunatic."

No reply and the voice on the other end went quiet.

"Listen....John. You're wrong."

"Am I?" he asked. "Are you one hundred percent sure that the man they arrested killed those people, or maybe...just maybe, Edward Munz was just a man smitten with Glynis and you didn't try hard enough to identify the real killer's face."

His words made me pause. My letter from years ago was about a stalker following Glynis. I hadn't claimed he was a serial killer. It was the FBI that had determined those facts. Had they made a mistake, or was this guy just trying to stall in a last-ditch attempt for a stay of execution?

"What proof do you have?" I asked, glancing down at the letter.

"You have it in your hands," he answered before the line disconnected.

DEADLY BLISS

West

Chapter 8

West paced the porch at the Lady Blue Plantation where Harrison and Nunnery were seated. This house had witnessed its share of love and laughter, and just as many crimes, which Cree and her father had tried to solve. This had been home to the Blue family for generations, and now it was absorbing copious amounts of tension and worry into the solid walls.

"We should have followed her," Nunnery said.

"We couldn't risk it," Harrison answered.

"She would have given you both the slip," West said, earning skeptical looks from both of them.

"Cree is a baker," Nunnery argued.

He could argue all he wanted. He didn't know Cree the way West did. "She's my wife. She would have lost you. I'd lay money on it."

West ran his hands through his hair and left them resting on the top of his head. "Who gets the antidote? Glynis or the President?"

They both looked at him like his question was taboo.

Harrison lowered his gaze to his hands, and Nunnery remained quiet. West had his answer. West and Cree were going to need to find the rest of the meds if there was any hope of Glynis getting what she needed. "I see."

The lights from Cree's Jeep illuminated the yard, and it wasn't until she stepped out unscathed that West breathed his first sigh of relief.

Cree parked the car and got out with a package in her hand. Her face was marred by a frown, and he would do anything if he could take this burden from her and fix it himself.

"Is that the package?" Nunnery asked, rising to his feet.

"Yes, I haven't opened it yet."

"Well, what are you waiting for?" Harrison asked.

West pulled out a knife for her to use when Cree's worry-riddled gaze met his. She shook her head.

"I need permission to see someone in jail."

"Fine," Nunnery said, trying to take the package from her hand, but she yanked it away.

"Federal prison, about to be executed." She glanced from West to Harrison. "There was a reason he gave you a deadline."

"Cree, you aren't making sense." West took her by the arm and guided her to sit in the swing. "Tell us what happened."

"I got the package and saw a letter in the same handwriting, so I took both." She gazed down at the package. "When I got back to my Jeep, my phone rang." She lifted her gaze to Harrison's. "It was him."

"He called you?" West asked.

Cree nodded. "He claims that Edward Munz wasn't the serial killer, only Glynis' stalker, and the FBI made a mistake."

Confusion clouded Harrison's face. "We found him in the trophy room where he kept all of the stuff from the victims."

This wasn't happening. West rested his elbows on his knees. "He wants you to prove it." He glanced sideways at Cree. "He wants you to find the right guy."

She nodded.

"A jury of his peers found him guilty," Nunnery offered.

"I didn't say I believed him, but what if he's telling the truth? What if Munz didn't kill all of those people and the killer is still out there? What if—"

Harrison held up his hand and paused before speaking like he was taking his time to formulate the right words. "You were the one who sent me the letter. You handed him over to us on a silver platter. We found him with the evidence."

"I warned you about Glynis' stalker." She shook her head. "I never told you he was a serial killer, only that he might harm her."

"What does this have to do with anything?" Nunnery asked, holding out his hand for the package.

"Everything." West rose from his seat. This guy had sent only one vial of antidote. One. In order for them to save Glynis and the president's son, Cree and West needed to find the truth. Finding a mad scientist was one thing, but a serial killer who'd perfected his kills and eluded law enforcement was a whole different game.

"The president isn't going to issue a stay of execution for a serial killer," Nunnery said and pointed at Harrison. "The FBI built a solid case against this guy."

Cree rose from her seat and handed Nunnery the package. He went to take it, and she jerked it back spitefully. Nunnery's eyes narrowed into aggravated slits at her antics. It worked. She finally handed it over to him. "I guess that leaves me less than seven days to uncover the truth and save Glynis and the president's son. John won't give us the vials if we don't."

"John?" Harrison asked.

"Yeah, that's what he told me to call him. Personally, I preferred raging lunatic, but some men are kind of funny about pet names I pick. I should have called him a zombie. That's what he really was. A dead man walking. Why is it I always come up with better comebacks when the moment is already gone?"

West grabbed Cree's hand and slid his fingers through hers. "Gentleman, if you're finished with the reasons you kidnapped my wife, then we're done here." He gazed into Cree's tired blue eyes. The weight of the world lay on her shoulders. A weight he had every intention to help bear. "My wife needs rest. God knows in the next six days she isn't going to get any."

She walked to the door, only pausing when Harrison rested his palm on her arm. "How can I help? You have the backing of the entire FBI at your disposal."

She gave him a sad smile. "Go spend time with your daughter. I'll figure this out. I have to."

Cree wasn't one to doubt, but West could read it in her eyes. She was going to hunt for a man that none of the other agencies had ever caught. It was an impossible task, but she wouldn't be going alone. If it were up to West, she wouldn't be going at all.

Cree made it to the door before she turned back to Nunnery. "What did you find at the address?"

"A dead rose," he answered. He slid the phone out of his pocket, pulled up a picture, and turned it to show her. A rose dipped in blue. He scrolled to the next picture, where words were painted on the wall. *Here lies your first clue.*

"This John guy isn't telling us everything he knows," West said.

"Don't worry. I plan to know it all." Cree patted West on the chest before disappearing inside the house.

"West," Harrison called out, stopping West from following Cree. He pulled out the empty vial that they'd used to prolong Glynis' life. "Maybe this will help her tap into finding the guy with the antidote."

"Thanks," West said, holding the empty vial between his fingers. Not a single drop of substance was left inside.

"If she discovers we got the wrong guy, tell her that I'll make it right."

There wouldn't be a need. If West got his hands on this killer or the scientist, neither would be alive to talk unless it was from the grave.

"You can't promise that," Nunnery protested.

"The president and his son might say otherwise," Harrison answered, holding West's gaze.

He was right. Even if what they had could cure the president, his son was still at risk. Still, it wouldn't matter considering the harm West was going to inflict. "Thanks."

"Remind me again, under whose watch did the president, his son, and Glynis get sick?"

Nunnery clenched his jaw. West already knew the answer but wanted to drive home his point. "So Cree is essentially cleaning up the Secret Service's mess."

"Now wait a minute," Nunnery objected.

West shrugged and left them both on the porch. He had better things to do, more important things. He found Cree standing at the doorway to their bedroom. Her arms were folded over her chest.

"He was in here."

"Not anymore," West announced, wrapping one arm around her and dangling a smashed electronic bug for her to see. "Freddie swept the entire house for us, but I did the bedroom right when we got back. I found two in here, and he found five more downstairs."

She shook her head. "I feel violated. Who would do that?"

West took her by the hand and led her into the room, closing the door behind him. She may have felt violated, but he was pissed. "Freddie is betting it was the electrician that you called when the circuit breaker tripped and wouldn't turn back on. My bet is on one of the temp guys that

Charlotte hired to help cook in the kitchen."

Cree met his gaze. "Will you find him if Nunnery and Harrison can't?"

"I'll do more than that, luv." He rested his palms on her cheeks. His lips hovered near hers. "I'll destroy him."

"You always know the perfect thing to say."

He'd keep all the details about how this man would suffer to himself. No sense giving her new ideas to try on her own.

"That's going to have to wait though. I have a wife in need of a bubble bath to help her destress." He kissed her lips. "I'll even help wash your back, Mrs. Archer." Not that he had any intention of stopping there.

"If I'd known marrying you came with perks, I might have done it sooner."

DEADLY BLISS

West

Chapter 9

Cree was sipping coffee in the kitchen when West finally meandered down the stairs. It was sweet she'd let him sleep, but they had too much to do to waste time.

"Good Morning, Mrs. Archer."

She smiled. "Blue-Archer."

"As long as you're my wife, I don't care which name you pick."

He smiled and kissed her before grabbing a coffee cup, pouring the black gold all the way to the rim. Cree hated black coffee. She liked more of a dash of coffee with her cream. He took his first gulp, hoping the caffeine would soon kick in.

"How long have you been up?" he asked.

"Three coffee pots."

"That's impressive."

Her eyes sparkled with mischief. "Well, I needed to work through all of the pros and cons of different ways to handle this. I've also made a list of 101 ways to destroy John, including how we'll get rid of each body part. You're welcome."

"Your little OCD mind has been busy."

"Harrison is bringing me some of the evidence from the serial killer file so I can use it to tap into the energy, but we both know I only have energy for one, and time isn't on our side."

He slowly nodded and listened to her ramble like any good husband would. When she pulled out the meat tenderizer and described how she was going to hurt John, it was West's dedication his husbandly duty to try and reel her back in.

"Let's find him first. Then you can smash all of his bones, luv." Not that she'd get the chance. He put the kitchen gadget back into the drawer.

"Doc Stone will be here in two hours with everyone else so I can use Insight. I still can't figure out how we can work both angles. We need to find the maniac who has the antidote, but I also need to find the real killer if it's not Munz. We can't let Glynis or her stalker die if he didn't commit the crimes."

"You know how to do both. Roni has been begging to use Insight. She'd do one of the sessions."

He was right, even if Cree wasn't ready to admit it. Cree wasn't the kind who liked to ask for help, and the kind of help she needed was dangerous. "She's just a kid."

"I am not," Roni said, walking into the kitchen.

"Eavesdropping on your elders isn't very adult-like," Cree smirked.

"Hey, I live here. If you want to have a personal conversation, do it elsewhere, and furthermore, you don't even have to ask. I'll help. I'm in, and before you tell me no, remember that I can always help you track down the killer instead of the sleazy blackmail guy. The choice is yours."

"Who told you about the sleazy blackmail guy?" Cree gawked.

Roni smiled but never answered.

West covered his smile, lifting the cup back to his lips as Cree sighed. Roni would follow them. It was as much in her genes as it was in Cree's. They were so much alike it was a little scary.

"Fine, but you're going first. That way I can watch and stop the session if things get out of control."

"You're such a mom." Roni chuckled and turned to leave, stopping at the last minute. She snapped her fingers and pointed at West. "Oh, I almost forgot. There's someone here to see you. I left them out on the porch."

"Who?" West asked. *Please don't be Parnell.* West hadn't had time to tell Cree that the man had called last night to offer his assistance. West hadn't even decided if he'd need it.

"Tall guy, kind of sexy for an old dude, oh and he talks like yours."

Bloody hell. He squeezed Cree's hand. "Did I forget to mention someone might stop by?"

"This isn't exactly an ideal time for social visits," she argued. "And how does this person even know we're in town? We should have been on our honeymoon."

"He's an old friend that offered to help." Cree was going to have their marriage annulled if not kill him first. He thought he'd have time to prepare her for who was waiting on the veranda. It was too late now.

"Because we both know how much I enjoy your friends," Cree answered, following West through the house to the front door.

"This one is different." West had to admit that Cree was right, however. She didn't like any of the few friends of his that she'd met. He couldn't fault her. The ones she'd met had almost got her killed.

Parnell Moody stood on the veranda with his back to the door, scanning the surrounding trees. He was always on alert. It was ingrained in him. To anyone watching, he looked like a businessman in his tailored suit. Only West knew better. Beneath the facade lurked a well-trained operative.

"Cree." West squeezed her hand. "I'd like you to meet Parnell Moody. Parnell, this is my wife, Cree."

Cree smiled politely, but West knew better. She was mildly annoyed by this interruption. She held out her hand. "It's a pleasure to meet you."

"The pleasure is all mine." Parnell shook her hand slightly, tilting his head in West's direction. "You haven't told her?"

"Told me what?" Cree asked.

"How did you know?" West asked. "She's said a total of six words to you."

"Told me what?" Cree's echoed question was a little more demanding.

Parnell slid his hands into his pockets. His look turned sincere. "I hear you're hunting a killer and a maniac. MI-6 is at your service."

Her mouth parted as she turned to West. "You called in backup?"

"Not quite, but if I would have, it would have been Parnell. He's the best," West said.

"I'm sorry you had to come all this way. But we don't need you," Cree said through a strained smile before turning to walk back inside.

Parnell rocked on the balls of his feet. "That's too bad. I've already hacked the local street cameras and discovered who deposited the package with the vial of antidote."

"You told him about that?" Cree spun around, and anger darkened her face.

"He didn't," Parnell answered. "Malcolm Nunnery did, although I was a bit surprised that West didn't come to me first. It wasn't until I called him and offered my assistance that he relented and allowed me to crash your party."

Cree crossed her arms over her chest. "So you caught the guy already?"

"Not yet. He's a tricky bloke. I monitored his next movements through the street cams to a warehouse, and when I arrived, it was empty. I never saw him leave."

Cree huffed. "Did you check the basements?"

"Every square inch. Would you like to see who it is that is playing mind games with you?"

"Do ghosts walk through walls?" Cree asked.

Parnell's brows dipped.

"She means yes," West answered.

Parnell pulled out his phone and punched a few buttons and handed it to Cree.

The color slowly drained from Cree's face. Her breathing became shallow as she stared at the phone without moving. She knew who this creep was. He didn't even need to ask. West slid the phone from her hands to take a look.

The guy had short-cropped brown hair. Military style. His build was a bit on the stocky side, about six foot if not a bit shorter. He didn't look like the brainiac scientist type West was expecting.

"You know him, don't you?" Parnell asked. "I can see it on your face."

"Tweedledum," she answered.

"Tweedle who?" West asked. He'd never heard Cree refer to someone with that nickname, but it was exactly the kind of name that he'd expect her to use for someone she didn't like.

"FBI Special Agent Samuel Hunter," Cree answered, slipping out her phone and dialing a number. "This is ten times worse than I thought."

Cree put the phone on speaker and sat on the swing. Slowly rocking it back and forth, she waited. Deputy Direction Harrison Reed answered on the third ring.

"Hey, Cree."

"Harrison, quick question."

"Sure."

"You remember those first two agents, Tweedledee and Tweedledum that you sent to find me after I mailed you the letter?"

West folded his arms over his chest and shared a confused look with Parnell.

"Sure, Fernandez and Hunter," He answered. "Why, what about them?"

"Whatever happened to them? Are they still working with the bureau?"

"Fernandez is, but Hunter got screwed up the head after almost dying. He couldn't pass the psych evaluation, so he quit."

Great, this guy Hunter was trained by the best and now mentally unstable. Even if they could find him, would he give them what they needed?

Cree clenched her eyes closed and visibly swallowed. "Does Hunter have any link to medicine or chemistry?"

There was a pause on the line. "If I remember correctly, he had a degree in forensic science with a minor in chemistry. Why?" Harrison asked.

Perfect. A mad scientist with an expired license to kill. This was getting better by the minute.

"And what connection did he have with the serial killer case?"

"Every agent has the one case that haunts them. The serial killer case was his. He was never convinced we got the right guy. It got to the point of obsession."

"Shit." West's worst-case scenario was just realized. "That explains why he's convinced Munz isn't the killer."

"And why he's the one with the antidote," Parnell answered.

And how he knew what Cree was capable of and why he'd targeted her. There wasn't anything random about any of this. It was planned out and calculated. Hunter could have been working on this since the day Munz was convicted if not even early.

"I'm so sorry," Cree said into the phone. "Hunter is the one behind the poisoning and has the antidote. It explains how he knew about me."

The line was silent.

Parnell was looking at the picture on his phone. "I knew you recognized him."

"She saved his life," Harrison answered. "I have to alert the agency. Cree, he's dangerous. We trained him. Whatever leads you uncover, you call them into me to hunt down. West, Parnell, you two watch her six. Samuel Hunter knows where Cree lives, and I wouldn't put it past him to try and get to her."

"Understood," Parnell answered.

"That explains how he knew to bug the house. He sounds like a ticking time bomb. What is he going to do if Cree doesn't produce the results he wants?" West asked.

"He's a chemist. I'm sure he'll blow up our house," Cree answered.

DEADLY BLISS

Chapter 10

"Harrison, I'm going to find him."

"Cree, he needs to see that you're working toward finding the serial killer. If he suspects that you know who he is, then we lose the element of surprise."

"I can do both," I said, meeting West's gaze. "Even though we aren't related by blood, I consider you and Glynis my family, and family comes first, always."

"Cree, I'm ordering you not to engage—"

"You're breaking up, Director." Cree hissed and made a crackling sound before punching the button to end the call.

"You didn't expect that to be convincing, did you?" Parnell asked.

"That was her being polite," West answered. "Normally she wouldn't have even pretended."

I rose from my seat and patted Parnell's suit lapel. "Welcome to the loony bin. I hope you enjoy your stay." I slowly bit my lip as I studied Parnell from his designer suit to the guns bulging from beneath. He was going to stick out like a sore thumb if he stuck around. I glanced at West. "He needs to sign a non-disclosure agreement before the show."

Parnell gasped, seeming a bit agitated that I'd asked such a question.

"I have a direct line to your president and my queen. I have the highest clearance of all MI-6."

Secret spies were a funny bunch. They didn't play by the rules, they had the best toys, and most had a hidden agenda. I knew first-hand.

"Yeah but you're in Blue territory where things are a little different," I said, crossing my arms over my chest. "What's your secret agenda-spy guy?"

Parnell raised his brow.

"Don't play stupid. Each of you has one."

Parnell remained steadfast, not showing me any sign of weakness. No sweat on his brow as he continued to meet my gaze. "I can assure you that I'm only here to help."

Hmm-hmm. "If I find out different, not only will I conjure every ghost I know to haunt your ass, I'll join in when I die and go all poltergeist on you."

He huffed and glanced at West. "Is she for real?"

I slipped my fingers into my mouth and whistled. "You can come out, now."

Faraday rounded the house from the east with a shotgun and waved it in the air. Freddie rounded from the west shoving his Beretta back into his jeans, and Roni peeked out from behind Parnell's snazzy sports car waving her knife. Not a one of them had ever seen when Roni waved and smiled at me.

"Nice wheels. Although judging by the mud in your tires, I'd venture a guess that you're staying near the Crampton farm. They have loud roosters nearby, not an ideal place for sleeping."

"She's for real," West answered, tossing his arm over my shoulders. "And she's all mine. Bless her ever-lovin' crazy heart." He said with an exaggerated southern twang he hadn't yet mastered before kissing my temple.

I ignored the praise and flicked two fingers from my eyes to Parnell's. I didn't care where he was from. He was an outsider in my little corner of the world, and I was about to give him a glimpse of the wizard behind the curtain.

I shoved my elbow into West's side. "Next time warn me when you expect company. Although, his timing is perfect. He can help carry the hospital bed."

"Come again?"

****

Two hours later, skepticism still registered in Parnell's eyes as he stood across the room when the activities started. I paced like any good cousin would as Doc Stone slid the cap over Roni's head.

"Is this necessary?" she asked.

I rolled my eyes. "It's going to get worse," I answered and crossed the room. "Next comes the cold gel, the probes, and then monsters that can't be unseen. You don't have to do this."

"Yes, I do," she said, clasping the locket around her throat. Her Grams and mine, well, they were sisters, and in a way, Roni was a younger version of me. She had the ability in one of her fingers that had taken me a lifetime to figure out.

West stood by me as I ignored the thick apprehension in the room making it difficult to breathe. If this didn't work would I be able to survive back to back sessions?

"She'll do fine," he whispered, wrapping his arms around my waist.

"We're ready whenever you are," Charlotte called out, making the large plasma display monitor come to life.

"We've never done this," I whispered, squeezing West's arm.

"It's going to work," he whispered, pressing a tender kiss to my temple. "I can feel it."

At least he's optimistic. "Any signs of distress and you pull her out, Doc."

"Of course." He nodded, and after squirting each hole in her cap with the gel, he began to attach the probes.

I wanted to hold Roni's hand. To make her feel safe, but I knew better than to try.

Roni was fearless like that. "You just have to relax and whatever you see in your head from holding the vial will populate the screen. In your mind, you'll be where he is, but you'll really be here with us where it's safe."

"Relax, mom. I can do this." Roni breathed a slow, comforting breath.

"Hit the lights, Freddie," I called out. The room became shrouded in darkness. The only illumination came from the white glow of the heart monitor and the blinding plasma hanging from the wall. I nodded to Doc Stone.

"Let's hunt," I yelled out, glancing toward Charlotte to verify once more that the red blinking lights on the video recorder were running.

Chapter 11

I held my breath while handing Roni the vial. I couldn't shake this foreign mom-like protective instinct no matter how hard I batted it away. I couldn't help it. Her fingers tightened around the glass.

"Just breathe," I whispered. That was good advice. I exhaled like a pregnant woman fighting through a contraction.

"Just go away," she whispered back.

A face appeared on the screen. It wasn't the one we were looking for, but it was one that I recognized. The woman from Roni's locket. My grandmother's sister I never knew existed.

"Grams," Roni said as a tear slipped from her eyes and her lips trembled.

"It's okay. You'll get used to it," I whispered. "You don't have much time, Roni. I need you to focus on the vial."

I glanced at my watch. I was never on this end of things. I had no idea how long she'd be able to stay under, but judging from experience, it was never long enough.

The picture faded, and with it, one last fat tear slid down Roni's cheek. The monitor turned to darkness with a single light shining from a distance before the rest of the area tuned in.

Tweedledum was wearing a doctor's coat sitting inside a lab. It wasn't like a hospital lab, more of the homemade variety. Ex-Special Agent Hunter looked different than I remembered. The wrinkles on his face were deeper, the bags beneath his eyes were dark and puffy, and a five o'clock shadow covered his chin.

Roni turned her attention to the desk. A newspaper clipping of Munz was sitting near the keyboard. Next to that was a bag with the insignia of the Center for Disease Control was stamped across it. Hunter's face came into view as if he were looking right through Roni.

Roni's heart rate accelerated. I remembered the first time I thought a killer could see me. I'd been the same way. The mind has a hard time remembering that it's safe in the face of monsters.

"You're safe. He can't see you. You're doing good," I whispered, looking up at the monitor. Roni watched Hunter now as he held a vial up to the light. There was no sound from just spectator seats, something I hadn't realized that others couldn't experience when I worked a session. If he was talking, only Roni could tell.

Hunter shoved out of the chair, placing the vial in the box, I could imagine the squeaky tape noise as he pulled it from the reel to seal it shut. His gloved hands wouldn't leave a trace. I scanned the screen for anything that might tell me where this butthead was hiding. Anything that might give us a clue.

I left the bedside, moving closer to the screen, as if getting this new viewpoint would help me find him. The lab was made up of tables and beakers and scientific stuff. Takeout food sat on the counter next to a laundry basket of clothes. What in the world was this guy doing?

He shrugged out of his lab coat. The guns in both arm holsters were hard to miss. Perfect, the mentally disturbed psychopath was still carrying.

"Anyone recognize the building?" I asked out loud.

I was answered with a chorus of no's.

"It looks like any one of the abandoned warehouses in the downtown district," Freddie answered.

We all continued watching as Hunter left the building.

"You can follow him," I said out loud so Roni could hear, and as she moved to step, the screen changed to a picture of Damien down on one knee with a engagement ring in his hand.

Well, it appeared my little cousin was just as good at keeping secrets.

I motioned to Doc Stone to pull her out of Insight. A few more steps. If she'd just followed him outside, we would know exactly where he was hiding. Roni opened her eyes. "I'm so sorry. I..."

"It's okay," Her eyes drooped closed as I layered on the blankets to fight her shivers. "You did great. You're going to sleep now. Don't fight it. You're safe."

She nodded just as her head lolled to the side. She was going to sleep for hours to recuperate, and even then she'd feel like she'd been on an all-night bender. Using Insight was draining in more ways than one. Not only on the user's energy but it also frayed the edges on their faith in humanity. She might not have witnessed a killer in the act, but she'd find out soon enough just how much evil thrived in our world.

A dim glow illuminated the ballroom. West, Parnell, and Freddie stood huddled, talking in hushed tones, forming plans that I doubted they'd share with me.

Charlotte was waiting as if she could read my mind. A smile split her lips as I crossed the room and rested my hand on the back of her chair. "Five bucks I find him first."

She grinned. "I'd never bet against you."

"Can you play it back for me?"

"I have it queued to go."

I'd analyze the crap out of each frame looking for a clue. There was never a flashing sign saying, *killer is hiding here.*

A few keystrokes later and the computer monitor started with a flash of Roni's grandmother's face, and I watched it again. Twice, before asking Charlotte to move frame by frame.

Faraday and Frankie had left the room to grab a town map to make a grid to chart their warehouse search. I was running out of time to prove I was smarter.

I pulled up a seat next to Charlotte and watched the video again, asking Charlotte to pause it when Roni had been looking at the desk.

A smile split my lips as I tapped the screen. "There."

Charlotte frowned. "What?"

"The Styrofoam container is from Markum's Diner. They're the only people that still use those things. Everyone else in town uses plastic. All we need is the postmark on the date the original vial was sent, and we can pull street cams."

I shot off a text to Harrison to ask, and he replied instantly. Thursday one week prior.

"Can you hack the street cams near Markum's Diner from Thursday?"

"Sure."

The keys clacked as Charlotte finessed her way into the CCTV system and after picking the right date, she had a video feed of the diner. Not knowing if it was night or day when he sent it, I pulled my seat closer as Charlotte, and I watched until I spotted the ex-special agent. I pointed to the screen. "That's him."

He picked up his food and walked out of frame.

Charlotte was good, better than anyone gave her credit for. She hacked the street light cams, and we watched as Hunter made his way down Main Street and turned into the old warehouse district. He came to one of the doors and glanced both ways before disappearing down a side alleyway.

"We've got him," I said to the others. My words went ignored until I whistled to get their attention. They turned to look at me. "We got him."

I crossed the room and pointed to the map. "He went down this alleyway after he picked up his takeout. He's in one of these two buildings."

"How do you know where he ordered from?"

"Because she's good." West kissed my lips. "Did I mention that she's mine?"

DEADLY BLISS

West
Chapter 12

West shot off a text to Harrison to tell them what they'd discovered before kissing Cree and heading out the door. They had a plan now. They had backup. West, Parnell, and Faraday were going to meet Malcolm Nunnery and his team three blocks away from the warehouse in one of the parking garages.

They were joking about who was going to shoot first when West reminded them that the vials of antidote and any traces of the formula were more of a priority than catching Hunter. Hunter, they could find again, but if they screwed this up, the antidote might be lost forever.

Nunnery rested a handheld military computer on the hood of the SUV. A live satellite feed was on the display. There was only one human-sized heat signature inside the old building.

"That's him. Our target is on the third floor. Alpha team 1, you take the front. Alpha team 2, you'll go up the fire escape and descend from the roof. West, you and your guys can cover the fire escapes and stay out of our way."

Out of their way? They wouldn't know which way to go if it hadn't been for Roni and Cree. Parnell gave West a sideways glance as if he'd read his mind. They were more than trained to take point and enter the building without being detected, and he'd be lying if he denied the thought hadn't crossed his mind on the drive over.

They dispersed through the alleyways three blocks up as the others left to round the blocks and approach from the back. This wasn't some crazy lunatic that wouldn't see a military hit team coming. They must have forgotten that Hunter had the same training as the rest of them, but West didn't forget.

Hunter had tracked down Cree from only a single letter a year ago.

"They're out for blood, mate," Parnell said as they followed out the doors.

"He's going to smell them coming," West said. "This guy is good considering Harrison originally hand-picked him to find my wife."

Unease slid down West's spine. It wasn't like finding him had come easy, but it still felt as though they were all walking into some elaborate game without being given the rules.

West and the others took up position in the alley across the street to keep an eye on the fire escapes as the other team slid against the building, giving them cover from any prying eyes.

"We should be the ones going in," Freddie grumbled.

"They're the ones carrying the badges," Faraday said.

West let them argue the merits of staying out versus being the ones to go in while he scanned the windows of the third floor. A single light illuminated one of the windows on that floor, yet there was no movement inside.

West's phone vibrated. A text from Cree. *Well???*

They're entering the building now. I'll text you when it's over.

No need. Look to your left.

He peeked out of the alley and turned his gaze down the street to find Cree in another alley, waving her phone at him.

Go home.

Not a chance. She answered with a skull and crossbones emoji.

West returned his gaze to the window just as a team was rappelling down the building and getting into position above the windows.

Faraday and Freddie's conversation cut off as they joined him in watching.

"This is stuff you only see on TV," Freddie whispered.

"You couldn't pay me a million bucks," Faraday answered.

"It's not that bad," Parnell offered. "I've done it from a high-rise."

Screamed shouts started as those rappelling kicked off the building and used their feet on the glass to break windows. Smoke from smoke grenades billowed out of the openings, rising into the night sky.

"Well, they sure know how to make an entrance," West said.

Nunnery appeared in the window and motioned they could come up. He wasn't there. No matter how much West hoped it ended here, he knew it wouldn't down in his core. No way would the ex-FBI agent not have a contingency plan.

They'd jogged across the street to enter the building when West glanced over his shoulder to find Cree still standing in the alley with the phone to her ear.

At a safe distance was exactly where she needed to be. Even if it was a bit unusual that her curiosity wasn't leading the way after the all clear.

West entered the abandoned building. It was similar in setup to the one that he and Cree had been in when they'd been searching for Faraday's brother. Trash and broken furniture littered the ground. It smelled old and musty. Dust covered every square inch of the furniture that wasn't broken. One of Nunnery's guys was holding open the stairway doors. "Third floor."

West took the stairs two at a time to the third floor where another agent was standing guard at the door as West and the others entered.

The remaining fog from the smoke was thick and burned his eyes. A single man was kneeling with his hands on top of his head in surrender.

"You can't arrest me I haven't done anything." The man coughed, blinking hard through the haze.

"Who is that?" Freddie asked.

West shrugged. He'd never seen the guy before, but West knew who it wasn't. Hunter was nowhere to be seen.

"Meet Theodore Munz," Malcolm announced, flipping the wallet closed. "So, Theodore, you going with the same alibi as your brother? Wrong place at the right time?" Nunnery asked, slapping cuffs on the man and yanking him to his feet.

"Where is Hunter?" West asked.

Theodore raised his brow, and a smile split his lip. "I don't know. He told me to wait here for him, and he stepped out about ten minutes before you guys showed. It was almost like he knew you'd be coming."

Anger rolled in West's gut. Had they missed one of the bugs at the house? That was the only way Hunter could have been warned.

"Sir...take a look at this." One of Nunnery's guys pointed at computer screens across the room.

Six monitors were set up. Three showed various angles from the woods around the Lady Blue Plantation, including one that was aimed at the driveway under the iron gate. The other three showed various street views downstairs. First the bugs and now cameras. Cree wouldn't get another restful night sleep if she knew.

The thought had faded from his mind when his entire body froze. Hunter was in a nearby alley, and he had Cree. How in hell did that happen? "Shit."

West ran for the door to the shouts of the other men. By the time he got to the alley, Cree was gone, and the only things that remained were her watch, her phone, her favorite knife, and a wand used by security in airports.

DEADLY BLISS

Chapter 13

"Well, that didn't take you long." Hunter chuckled into the phone.

"Let me guess. You aren't in there," I said angrily.

"No, but I'm closer than you think. Simply turn around." Hunter chuckled again, ending the call.

I spun around to find Hunter aiming a gun at my chest, the barrel black and lethal. He slid the phone into his pocket. "So we meet again."

"I warned you I was coming for you."

I'd taken a step back to make a run for it when Hunter pulled two vials from his pocket, stopping my attempted escape. "If you want these, I need you to come with me."

I glanced at my watch and tried to hide the smile. That smile was short-lived when Hunter pulled a wand out of his back pocket and held it up. "Leave your trackers and weapons behind, and no funny business or I'll destroy the antidotes here and now."

I took the hat from my head and pulled the watch off my wrist. I set the items down by my feet before adding my phone.

"Give me the vials." I held out my hand.

"Not yet." He turned the wand on, running it in front of my, stopping at my ankle. He stepped back. "Why am I not surprised you didn't listen?"

He threw one of the vials at the brick wall, breaking the glass. The liquid inside splattered, making my heart clench. *Brilliant, Cree. Piss off the crazy guy.*

"Wait." I held out my hand, stopping him from throwing the other one. "I forgot I had it. Just wait."

I slowly bent down and pulled out the knife from my leg holster and tossed it inside the hat. "That's everything. Do your wand thingy and then give me the vial."

"Turn around," he ordered, and I complied, slowly turning my back toward the maniac.

The wand made funny noises as it was waved over my body. He reached around me and waved it in front of me, and it started beeping at my pocket.

"It's just my car keys."

Hunter reached into my pocket and pulled out the keys with the keychain of mace and tossed it to land with the other things in the hat.

"I'm innocent like Munz," he whispered into my ear. Goosebumps shivered over my body from head to toe. He was telling the truth.

"I've left my personal files waiting for you at your old house." His lips twitched. "Your fake house with the neighbor killer from when we met. Find the connection between the victims, and you'll understand."

He took my arm to lead me down the alleyway and away from the building that Nunnery had raided. A car was parked on the street with the door open. He let me go and rounded the car with his gun pointed in my direction.

"Find the connection."

"Wait...the vial," I yelled.

His lips twisted at the corner, and he tossed the antidote in the air.

I caught it with both hands.

"Find the connection and don't trust anyone. Not everyone is who they seem."

Goosebumps. He knew more than he was telling me.

"I need more time. I could work this case a lot faster if you told me everything you know. Why all the secrecy? Who shouldn't I trust?"

He shook his head. "In five days, this will all be over, one way or another."

I watched helplessly as he sped off and only turned toward the sound of thumping feet hitting the pavement. Sliding the vial in my pocket, I rounded back into the alleyway and headed toward West. Nunnery and his merry men with guns drawn sped past me.

"You just missed him," I called out.

"What the hell happened? Did you warn him that we were coming?" Nunnery growled.

"What the hell are you talking about? If it wasn't for Cree, you wouldn't have known where to look," West argued. His face pinched in anger. This was a side of

West I didn't see often, but it was kind of turning me on.

Nunnery let out an aggravated breath and shoved his gun in his holster. "What happened? What did he say?"

"He said you're an asshole," I improvised with a smile. "He offered me the vials if I went with him. He threw one against the brick when I told him to go to hell."

"What!" Nunnery's jaw dropped. "Let me get this straight. You didn't comply, and he destroyed one of the vials? Are you fucking insane?"

"If you want the vials, you follow him and get in the car with the crazy psycho. I still have a murderer to catch, and I can't do that if my dead body is dumped on the side of the road."

Nunnery closed the distance between us. The chemicals from the gas canister lingered on his clothes, making me sneeze. Was his angry glare supposed to intimidating?

"You killed your friend by not getting in that damn car."

"You're just mad he's smarter than you. He got the drop on your little sting and left you looking like a joke."

West took my arm and inched in front of me, getting right into Nunnery's face. He shoved against his chest. "You want to blame her for the Secret Service's screwup?" West shoved him again. "You need to look in the mirror, asshole."

My money was on my husband. "Get him, tiger."

"Back off or she walks and good luck explaining *that* to the president."

Parnell stepped between the two, strong-arming each of them to give the other some space. "Everyone just calm the hell down. He didn't have time to destroy everything. I'm sure we'll salvage the antidote formula on his computer."

Nunnery glared at me, pointing an accusing finger in my direction. If he kept it there, I was going to bite it off.

"You better hope for Glynis' sake that he's right."

I raised a brow in challenge. "Or you'll what? Charge me with not helping you? Good luck making that stick. I'm sure the press would be very interested to know you need the help of a psychic. Asshat."

I grabbed West's arm and spun him around to head back where I'd left my stuff. If they for one minute thought that I had the vial, it would be whisked away and used on the president's son. Not that I wished him ill, but I wished Glynis better more. No way was I going to let Nunnery chose who would live longer. It was my choice, I'd done the work.

West slid his fingers through mine with one last angry glare over his shoulder. "Are you really okay?"

I nodded. "I'll be better when I find the killer. Hunter told me not to trust anyone. He knows more than he's telling us."

"Okay, so we'll find the killer."

I stopped to grab my things. "It was weird. He knew I was armed, but he didn't try to hurt me. He said he's innocent and everything isn't as it seems."

"Did you believe him?"

I held out my arm to show West my still visible goosebumps. Hunter had been telling the truth. The question was, if he knew the answers, why in the hell was he playing this game?

"Let's get you home."

"We have to go see Glynis before I get started."

"Why Glynis?"

I grinned. "I'll tell you about it in the car. You want to ride with me?"

"Oh yeah. You aren't going anywhere without me. Not after that." West took out his keys and tossed them to Freddie. "Can you take the guys and my car back to the house? Cree and I will meet you there."

Chapter 14

I wiggled my fingers in passing at the guards giving entry to the house where Glynis was being kept. Director Reed met us at the door. "You found his lair."

"We did."

Harrison's brows dipped as he gazed down at my empty hands. "Did you give the antidote to Nunnery?"

Funny he should ask that question. Why would he think we had? Hopeful? I raised my brow. "Why would you ask that?"

Harrison's lips parted. "Well, you found his lair, right?"

"Right, and, no, Nunnery doesn't have it. I do."

"What? Why didn't you give it to him?"

"Because I'm not letting that douche decide Glynis' fate. She is." I sidestepped the director and headed toward Glynis' room. As if West could read my mind, he pulled Harrison away to discuss something else, giving me time to slip inside the door. The nurse wasn't at her post, but Glynis was where I'd left her. She smiled as I neared.

"Two visits. I'm a lucky girl."

I took her hand and sat at her bedside. "I have some good news."

Her worried gaze held mine. "You found the real killer?"

She coughed and grabbed the mask, holding it to her face. I hated seeing her like this. So weak and frail. This wasn't the Glynis that I knew. The spunky girl who'd introduced me to her famous friends.

"Not yet but I will." I slipped the vial out of my pocket and held it between my fingers. "This might be the only other antidote in existence. Hunter destroyed the other one."

A frown slid onto her face as Glynis slowly pushed into a sitting position. She took the vial from my fingers and cupped it in her palm.

"Only one?"

"For now, unless I find the killer," I answered.

She lifted her gaze to mine and handed me back the vial. "Danny is more than just the president's son, Cree. He's the love of my life."

"Think about what you're saying."

"I have." Glynis swallowed hard. "I choose him." She glanced down at the vial in my hands. "Give it to Nunnery to take to Danny."

"Any way I can force you to be selfish?"

She shook her head and grabbed my hand, closing my fingers around the container. "Even if you don't find the real killer and get another antidote, I'll survive this. I'm resilient that way. I made the choice, and I chose him."

I lowered my gaze to hide the tears welling up in my eyes.

"You would have done the same thing for West. That's what makes us special, Cree. When we love, we love with everything we've got. They're lucky men."

A single tear escaped, slipping free as I lifted my gaze to hers. "Don't give up on me. I'll get you the antidote."

"Find the killer, Cree."

I heard Nunnery's voice on the other side of the door, and Glynis motioned with her head. She was right. I'd do the same thing for West. I slowly rose from the bed as the door flew open.

Nunnery's face hardened. "Why did you come back here? Why aren't you looking for Hunter and the killer?"

I held out the vial in passing as I headed for the door. "Why are you still here?"

He took it and glanced from me to Glynis. "He gave this to you, and you were going to save Glynis?"

"She is my friend. I let her choose, not you, and she chose Danny, so go fire up your chopper, or whatever it is that you do, and save his life while I continue to try and save hers." I walked into the other room and met West's gaze. I slowly shook my head and pushed out my bottom lip.

"I'm sorry, Cree."

"Sorry about what?" Harrison asked.

"She wouldn't take it," West answered.

"We'll be in touch." I squeezed Harrison in a tight hug before following West out the front door.

DEADLY BLISS

West

Chapter 15

Cree was in the kitchen again when West woke up and headed downstairs. He followed the delicious smells filling the air. His stomach growled in appreciation. Cree did some of her best thinking when she was working out recipes. It was one of her best quirks, regardless of the new ten pounds he'd put on since meeting her. He'd just push a little harder in his workouts to stay fit.

"Something smells wonderful," he said as he rounded the corner to find Cree overstuffing a picnic basket full of containers. "Uh...do you think this is the best time to take a picnic, luv?"

"You'll thank me when you're hungry later." She slid her watch off and laid it on the counter along with her phone and then held out her hand. "Where's your phone?"

West pulled it out and handed it to her. "What's wrong with yours?"

"Nothing. Hunter warned me not to trust anyone, so I'm making us untrackable."

West slowly nodded. "Then I guess that means we're taking my car?"

"Actually, Faraday's truck." She grinned. "I put a tracker on your car like you did on mine. Can't have you going around and getting lost, especially with the friends you keep."

His mouth parted, making her grin. She grabbed the coffee can and two mugs and put them in a shopping bag before unplugging the coffee maker. She grabbed the bag and the coffee maker and grinned. "Grab the basket, big guy, and let's go."

"Where are we going?"

"To work."

"To work it is." He grabbed the basket, following behind the love of his life. Cree was full of surprises. Her thought process wasn't just outside the box; it was three planets over, making a move toward the sun. It was one of the things he adored about her.

West drove the big truck that was about three times the size of his sports car and ten times harder to turn. The sun was shining above, and it was a clear early morning where the birds were already chirping in the trees. He followed her directions, letting her point the way and finally pulling up into the drive of an unfamiliar house in a suburban neighborhood.

He turned the engine off and got out, following her lead. "Who lives here?"

She shrugged. "I don't have a clue."

His brows dipped. "So what's the plan? You just going to knock on the door and ask if they have a spare room?"

"We can try that," she said and did exactly that. She knocked on the door, and they waited, hearing the door being unbolted from the other side. When the door opened, they both took a step back.

Hunter was standing on the threshold. "It's about time. Come in."

Cree followed, but West was more leery. "Uh, Cree... he's the bad guy. What the hell is going on?"

"Hunter said nothing is as it seems and the files were in this house. So... I did some digging on my own. You knew that we still had surveillance links to this house from when I lived here. Didn't you?" Cree rested her hand on her hip.

Hunter remained mute, neither confirming nor denying the claim. His silence was enough confirmation.

"Of course you did. Funny when I checked the name on the deed it happened to be Gerti Lake."

"Wait...isn't that the name of the lake where Glynis and her dad meet in emergencies when they need to go off-grid?"

"Why, yes it is, honey." Cree smiled and never turned her gaze from Hunter's. "You knew that there were still surveillance cameras in this house. Surveillance I had access to."

No answer.

"You had to know I'd check it to make sure this wasn't a trap."

Hunter's lip twitched. "I thought you might."

Cree stepped around Hunter and into the house. "Imagine my surprise when I found Deputy Director Harrison Reed and you on that feed."

West followed Cree into the house and came face to face with Harrison Reed.

"Tell me this wasn't some twisted fucking game," Cree said, spinning around to face Hunter.

"You might want to sit for this." Harrison gestured to the couch.

"I can't wait to hear this," West said, tossing Hunter the keys to the truck. "Mind unloading Cree's things? She's going to need more coffee." If not something stronger.

Harrison crossed his arms over his chest. Gone was the black suit and tie along with the grieving, worried father façade. "The FBI got tipped off that there was going to be an attempt on the president's life."

"The poisoning?" Cree asked.

"Exactly."

"If it wasn't Hunter, then who?"

"Malcolm Nunnery," Hunter answered, carrying in the picnic basket. "We were tracking movement in the deep web black market. We came across the transmission that someone was looking for the exact poison that was listed in our tip."

"And you tracked it back to Nunnery?"

"Not at first. We found the chemist, who replied. It was through Munz that he told us it was Nunnery." Hunter answered.

"Pinning the serial killings on Munz was a convenient way to tie up that loose end. Kill two birds with one stone." Cree said.

"We still didn't have any physical evidence against him," Hunter answered.

"After confidential deliberation with the president, we switched the poison with a mild strain of the flu, knowing Nunnery had plans to spike their drinks."

"Glynis has the flu?" Cree asked. Her voice was hopeful.

"Yes, but we couldn't tell her or the president's son."

"You aren't going to win father of the year."

"She had to believe that the threat was real. We knew we hit pay dirt when Nunnery never showed at the White House with the first vial. He hasn't even told the president that he has the first one or the one from yesterday."

"You set him up?" West asked.

"We did," Harrison answered.

Cree rose from her spot. "Good job catching the creep, but I still don't understand what this has to do with Munz or me."

"Munz is innocent of the serial killings."

"Then what in the world is he doing in jail?" Cree rested her fist on her hips.

"He's staying put in solitary confinement until we nail Nunnery and his accomplice," Harrison answered. "Munz was the person who gave us the tip about Nunnery's plans. It was Nunnery who set Munz up to take the fall. It was a perfect plan. No one would believe a convicted serial killer. There was only one flaw."

"Which was?" Cree asked.

"The people who died weren't random."

"So you really do need me to find the killer?" Cree asked.

"You already did," Harrison answered. "We needed his accomplice, and Nunnery couldn't be in two places at once. He'd want to stick close to the investigation into Hunter to intercept what he believes is the cure."

"Your bogus investigation," West interrupted.

"Well, yes, our bogus investigation. But we needed Nunnery to believe that we were also intent on finding the real killer. He'd need eyes on Cree."

"You son of a bitch, you used her." West advanced on Harrison and grabbed him by his shirt.

"Parnell," Cree answered, grabbing West's arm to pull him away. "Parnell is the other player."

"What? No," West argued.

"You didn't call him. He called you. He said he was disappointed that you hadn't called him. He's the other player, but what I don't understand is what the end game is. What does MI-6 get out of this?"

"Not MI-6," West answered, stalking to the French doors to look outside. "He's the muscle. He takes the occasional odd mercenary-for-hire job."

"How do you know?" Cree asked.

"He tried to recruit me," West answered, turning around. "That was the business meeting I had."

"You didn't..." Cree asked, and a look of disappointment filled her eyes.

"No, luv. I didn't."

"Okay, so why am I here?" Cree asked. "You know Nunnery is trying to assassinate the president, although I still don't understand why."

"He's pushing the FDA for stronger drug reform and wanted them to start with the most recent ones. The Vice President is much more lenient with the corporations.

"Okay, fair enough. The President was in his way. But if you now know Parnell was the muscle, why not just arrest them both and be done with this charade?"

"That's where you come in," Harrison said, gesturing to the hallway. "We know how the deaths are tied together, but we don't have any real evidence that wasn't planted on Munz. We need proof that Parnell was involved."

Harrison stopped in front of the door I'd used as my bedroom when I'd stayed there. He opened the door and stepped back, letting them step in first. Moving boxes lined the walls, labeled "bedroom." Cree opened the first one to find evidence boxes inside with one of the victim's names. West opened another to find even more. "Everything you need to connect them to the killings is in these boxes."

"Wow," Cree whispered beneath her breath.

Wow was right. The evidence was overwhelming but not as much as the four whiteboards positioned around the room. Each had a picture of the victim with statistics, photos of their deaths, and words circled in red. No doubt the connection they had to each other.

West slowly walked around the room. A law clerk was on one board, a hospital ER nurse on another. A pharmaceutical rep on another. A prostitute on another. The prostitute's occupation made West pause.

"How is she connected?"

"The prostitutes name is Rose Black."

The first clue they'd found at the apartment. It made sense now.

"They're all connected to CUBE73. Nunnery's brother runs the company making it," Harrison announced, moving to the boards. "The pharmaceutical rep was going to expose the drug trails were failures. The law clerk was the one who discovered the inconsistencies when family members of the trial patients wanted to sue."

"The ER nurse then is understandable, but what about Rose Black?" West asked.

"We're not sure about her, yet. When we were reviewing the law clerk's files, we found her initials in the clerk's appointment book. They match the initials of one of the bodies connected to the killings."

"I'll start with her," Cree announced, turning back to the room.

"Why her?" Hunter asked.

"She's standing right there." Cree walked over to one of the boxes and opened it and then the evidence boxes inside. She looked to the side like she was looking at the wall; she was probably looking at the ghost.

"This?" she asked, pointing to an object.

Cree nodded and grabbed a different object from the box. "I'm going to need this." She stood to meet West's gaze. "In order for this to work, I'm going to need you to keep Parnell busy and away from the house so I can use Insight." She turned her gaze to Harrison. "And you have to keep eyes on Nunnery. If he gets wind that we know, he'll make a play for Glynis to keep you silent."

"What do you want me to do?" Hunter asked.

She shrugged. "I guess just keep being the bad guy."

DEADLY BLISS

Chapter 16

"That was sleazy," West announced while turning onto the long road that would take us home.

I understood his opinion, hell, I even agreed with it. I could even rationalize the reason why it was an important ruse to keep playing.

"It had to be done." My heart was a bit more at ease knowing that even if I failed finding the connection that Glynis wouldn't die. It was my only comfort considering that killers not only knew where I lived but were on a first-name basis with everyone I held dear.

These people wouldn't be in our lives if it weren't for me playing armchair detective with the big boys. Could I ever live with the fact that someone I loved wound up hurt or, worse, dead? Was it worth it? No.

I contemplated that question the entire ride back to the house. It ate at me, clawing like a worm digging in my brain.

"What do you want me to do with Parnell?" West asked, pulling me from my thoughts.

"Go do your boy spy things."

West glanced at me before slowing the truck to the side of the road. "Okay. I'll do my spy things if"—he threw the gear shift into park—"you tell me what's going on in that head of yours, or are you going to make me guess?"

I didn't know how to tell him.

"Cree, luv. You can talk to me," West said, taking my hand.

"It's over."

"Come on, I'm not that bad. We've been married less than a week."

I gave him a sad smile. "Not us, using Insight, chasing killers. I'm done."

"This is who you are."

"This isn't who I want to be. I want normal. The 2.5 kids." My brows dipped. "What is up with a half a kid? I never understood that saying. How about we just have three kids? I want to grow old with you, and at the rate I'm going, one of us is going to get to get hurt—or dead—before that happens." My gut twisted viciously."

West was silent.

"You want that too, don't you?" I asked, my gaze pleading with his.

He turned in the seat and took my other hand in his. "Listen to me. I love you. What I want is for you to be happy. If normal will make you happy, then I'll move heaven and earth to be the best normal husband I know how to be. I chose us, but I know that you can't turn off the ghost thing, and I know you have a huge heart and want to help people."

"I can't keep risking everyone's life," I said, ignoring the squeeze in my heart.

"Then you'll just find a safer way to help. You'll still be you, only happier. You can't turn off who you are because you're scared."

I narrowed my eyes.

"But you can change the circumstances and channel that big heart into something just as meaningful and less dangerous."

Meaningful and less dangerous. An idea was already starting to form in my head. "Still me. I might be able to think of something."

"I have no doubt." He leaned across the seat and kissed my lips. "Now, are you ready to save their asses one more time before you put them on notice that this is your last stand?"

"I was thinking I'd be more like riding off into the sunset." I waved my hands as if I could see the sun rising and a horse riding off in the distance.

West put the truck into gear and pulled back out on the road. "I'm with you riding or walking, luv."

"Hey, back at the rental house you mentioned that Parnell tried to recruit you. Have you figured out what you want to be when you grow up?"

West's laugh filled the cab, making me grin.

I turned back in my seat. "I mean, my dad and Grams left me money, but I'm not a sugar-momma-type girl. You have to earn your keep."

He took my hand and squeezed it. "Money will never be our problem."

I turned my gaze to his. "Yeah? Are you a closet millionaire?"

"Something like that."

"And here this whole time I was thinking that you spent all your money on fun spy toys, sports cars, and wild women."

"Once upon a time I did." He grinned. "But I'd never be able to spend it all in this lifetime."

I rubbed my hands together. "Our future kids thank you."

He laughed again as he turned into our driveway. He slowed to a stop behind my car and turned the ignition off. "So what's the plan?"

"First I need an idea of when." I took out my phone and dialed Doc Stone, only to have the message go to voicemail. "Hey, Doc, it's Cree. Can you call me back and let me know when you're available for a session?"

"Try him at the hospital," West said.

I dialed that number next and was put through to his office.

"Hello." A female voice I didn't recognize answered the phone.

"Hi, this is Cree Blue-West. Is Doc Stone around?"

"Oh sorry, you just missed him."

"Do you know when he'll be back?"

"He said something about a family emergency, and he was leaving town for a few days. I'm not sure when he'll be back. I can call his cell and give him a message."

"I already left one. Thank you." I hung up.

"Busy?" West asked.

"Gone," I answered, sliding out of the truck and grabbing the picnic basket that I'd packed.

"When will he be back?" West asked, grabbing the coffee maker.

"I'm not sure. Maybe we'll have to try to use someone else."

"There's another doctor?" West asked, walking alongside of me.

"I was thinking more like Faraday," I answered just as the door opened.

Faraday came walking out with none other than the one man I was hoping to avoid. He was patting Parnell on the back. "See, I told you they'd show up before you left."

"Parnell, what are you doing here, and where is your car?" West asked.

"He was coming to tell you bye when I spotted his car on the side of the road up the street." Faraday answered.

"You know those damn rental cars. They aren't very reliable."

Unease slid down my spine when no goosebumps rose on my arms.

Damn. A few more minutes and we could have avoided this altogether.

"Right. Well, I'm just going to go unpack the basket," I said, glancing over my shoulder and back at West. I gave him a slight shake of my head and mouthed, "no goosebumps."

"Could you take this in for Cree?" West asked, handing Faraday the coffee machine.

"Sure. I was just going to take Parnell back into town."

"I'll do it," West announced and handed Faraday his keys. "Your truck wasn't running right. Just let me go get the keys to my car."

Thank God my husband was smart. If anything were to happened on that drive, I would have never been able to track him.

I didn't like the thought of West being alone with Parnell knowing that he was the muscle for a man wanting to kill the president, but West could take care of himself.

I headed for the kitchen, and Faraday followed.

"I hope you have some leftovers. I'm starving," Faraday announced.

"I don't think you're going to like them...seeing how you aren't a termite," I answered, opening the basket and pulling out the evidence and files about the dead prostitute.

"Where did you get these?" he asked, flipping one of the files open.

I sighed. "It's a long story." I rested my hip against the counter. "Where was Parnell's car? We didn't pass it coming in."

"I went for a drive up to my old property to meet a realtor. Someone is interested in buying the land and rebuilding."

"So you didn't come from town?" I asked, knowing that Faraday's house was up in the woods near the lake.

"Nope."

"Huh, then where was Parnell coming from since he was coming from the wrong direction?"

"Beats me. The only thing up that way is some old abandoned farmhouses. So what's with the evidence bag and files?"

"The same thing it always is," I answered. "Looking for clues. Listen, you've seen Doc Stone when he sets me up to use Insight and work the monitors. Do you think you'd be willing to try for him?"

"Where's Stone?"

"Some type of family emergency. He left town."

Faraday rested his palm on my arm. "Cree, Doc Stone doesn't have any family still alive, and he was scheduled for surgery today. He'd never leave one of his patients."

"Son of a bitch," I yelled, running from the room. I yanked open the basement door and took the stairs three at a time. All the breath in my lungs expelled as I started yanking sheets from everything that was covered in the hope that Insight wasn't gone but merely stored in a different spot and not on top of the cart were we usually kept it.

"What's going...." Faraday asked, standing on the last step. "Hey, where's the machine?"

"He took it," I whispered, pulling out my phone to warn West.

Faraday pointed to the window. "Someone broke the window."

"Where's Roni?" I asked, still trying to punch in West's numbers.

"I took her over to Damien's house on my way to the property."

"Check on her. Make sure she stays put." I growled, waiting for West to pick up.

Faraday had his phone out and to his ear while I left a message. "He took Insight. Call me back."

Faraday held up his phone. "She didn't answer."

"Freakin' fracking, I know better than to trust outsiders to watch me use that damn machine," I muttered as I dialed Moreno's number.

"Well, Cree this is a nice surprise."

"Is Roni there?" I asked.

"No, she's with Damien. They went for a walk."

"Goddamn it. Can you call him and see where they are."

"They should be back anytime for lunch."

"Just do it and call me back, Moreno," I growled into the phone. "She's in danger."

I hung up and started to jog back up the stairs in search for Charlotte.

"Cree, wait."

I spun around to face him and started to blurt out everything I'd learned. "He was parked on the side of the road so we wouldn't see him. He stole Insight. He's the muscle for Nunnery in their plot to kill the president. Parnell is the hired help, and he's with my husband."

"Calm down, Cree. Even if Parnell took the damn machine, you still have the plans for it, and he can't use it without a psychic and Doc Stone."

"That's my point. The machine, Doc Stone... I need to find Roni and warn West."

"Assuming what you're saying is true, what use would they have for that machine?"

His question made me pause. What use would Parnell and Nunnery have for that machine? It only let me connect with the dead and to see the crimes. "I don't know."

"Then don't panic just yet. The only thing you know for sure is Doc Stone gave an excuse at work. I'll call the station and send someone by his house to do a welfare check and stop by the hospital to look for anything suspicious."

"Right," I said. "And be sure to check the security cameras for when he left, to make sure he didn't leave under duress."

I spun around and headed for the stairs.

"Charlotte's not up there," Faraday called out, stopping me in my tracks.

"Where is she?"

"She went to the store seeing how you cooked up everything edible in the house."

I dialed her number and sat on the stairs. When her voicemail answered, a growl rumbled through my chest. "Charlotte. I need you to come back to the plantation. It's an emergency. Just leave the groceries. I need you."

I hung up when my phone rang again, announcing Moreno.

I rose, grabbing the banister as I answered. "Tell me you have her."

"Damien didn't answer, so I sent one of my guys to go look for them. Cree, tell me what is going on."

For the first time in forever, I let the tears fall where they may. My whole body shook while telling Moreno that the people I loved most in the world were in danger because of me. At some point through my meltdown, Faraday took the phone and continued the conversation with a man he hated while I covered my face to muffle my uncontrollable sobs.

Chapter 17

I paced alone in the ballroom and muttered beneath my breath. "You better be right."

Harrison Reed was the voice in my ear. "He'll come. I told him we had a lead on Agent Hunter and that we discovered he took the serial killer files. He'll want to tie up his loose ends. He needs to know what we have."

He'd better be right. There were only two ways this dirtbag was leaving my house, assuming he ever showed—dead in a body bag or in a pair of silver bracelets riding in the back of an ambulance.

My gun sat heavy in the waistband of my jeans, my knives secure in the ankle strap. Charlotte had moved the computer upstairs and was running a trace on West's cell and his car while hunting down their movements from whatever traffic cams she could find.

"Look sharp," Freddie whispered over the comm. "Our company has arrived."

I inhaled a deep breath, fighting the urge just to pull my gun. Harrison had enough on Nunnery to take him down. The strategic location was my doing. My turf, my husband, my rules.

A knock sounded on the door, and I slowly answered it.

Nunnery glanced over my head. "Where's Harrison? He called and said to meet him here."

"Oh, he'll be back. Come on in. He asked that you wait for him."

He followed behind me into the kitchen where I poured a glass of freshly made lemonade and offered it to him. I silently watched as he guzzled half. I ignored my inner bitch's desire to grab a knife from the butcher block and de-man him.

"Would you like to see what I've come up with so far?"

"Sure." He followed me into the ballroom where I already had the prostitute's file up on the Plasma. I gestured to it. "She was the missing piece, the only person Hunter couldn't tie with the other serial killer deaths." I crossed my arms over my chest. "Kind of convenient the way they caught Edward Munz with all the evidence he kept."

I glanced at Nunnery. His face was tight, his lips pressed into a thin line.

"A little too convenient if you ask me." I pointed to the pictures of the others killed. "You'll never guess what they all had in common."

Nunnery swallowed as he turned to me. "What?"

"You," I said and tossed the empty vial at him. "How did that lemonade taste? Did it have a bitter bite to it?"

"I'll fucking kill you," he growled and went for my throat, lifting me in the air and slamming me into the ground. I brought my arms up through his grip on my neck using all of my force to break his hold and went straight for his eye sockets the way Freddie had taught me. No way was this guy going to win. He'd already tipped his hand.

The gun was pressed between the floor and my back. Nunnery turned his head in an attempt to fight the attack on his face. His strength waned. "What the hell did you give me?"

His fingers on my throat loosened as he fell to his side. I struggled to stand, rubbing the ache on my scalp from where it slammed hard onto the floor. "The same thing as Glynis, only a more potent dose."

Nunnery went to sit up, and I straddled him, restraining his arms as I pulled my gun and held it to his head, cocking the trigger. "Where is Parnell?"

No answer. So I did what any good pissed-off southern woman would. I decked him hard in the face until blood oozed from his mouth. "I won't ask again. The next time you get a bullet through the head."

"You won't kill me," Nunnery spat.

"She won't, but I will," Hunter said, moving into the room with Deputy Director Reed.

"And if he won't, then I will," Faraday said as he and Moreno entered behind them with guns drawn.

"Tell her what she wants to know, and I'll let them arrest you instead of letting my guys deal with you." Moreno growled taking a menacing step forward and giving them a deadly smile.

"I found him. I f..." Charlotte came running down the stairs. Her words trailed off as she slowed entering the room.

I wouldn't look away from Nunnery. I might have double dosed him with the flu, but I was still pretty sure he thought I was using the exact drug that he'd tried to give Glynis and not the one that was switched.

"Where is he, Charlotte?"

She shook her head, meeting my gaze. "The abandoned farmhouse up the road."

"How is the hooker tied to this?" I asked, and he didn't answer.

I held up another vial. "You'll tell me if you want to live."

"She was Parnell's girlfriend. She witnessed the murders and then ran off with his money and the pictures he took to prove the deaths."

Well, I hadn't seen that one coming. I yanked his Secret Service badge off his waistband, and he went for my throat again. A single shot sounded throughout the room, hitting Nunnery in his head. Blood splattered on my clothes from my straddled position. I glanced over my shoulder to find Harrison lowering his weapon.

"Was that necessary?"

"Yeah. It kind of was," he answered.

Harrison walked over and lifted Nunnery's sleeve where a knife was hidden and partially poking out. "He was going to stab you in the throat."

"Then I guess we're even." I grinned and slowly rose to stand and glanced at Hunter and Harrison. "You guys got this?"

"Yep."

I uncocked my gun and slide it back inside my jeans. "Moreno, you and your guys are with me. It's time I go get the rest of my family."

West

Chapter 18

"Tell me what she knows," Parnell growled before pain radiated through West's cheek. He could no longer try to hold back the grunts or open his left eye. Wet sticky blood mixed with sweat sliding down his face.

West remained silent, working at the knots binding his hands at the back of the chair.

"I knew you wouldn't break easy, but I'm sure they will," Parnell said, picking up the knife.

West peered from beneath his swollen eye as Parnell left the room, returning, first, with Doc Stone and then Roni, binding each to different chairs.

Roni was like a savage, trying to hurt Parnell if she found an opening. Kicking him and headbutting him each chance she got. Cree would have been proud if not a bit mortified. "I'm going to kill you when I'm free."

"She's a fighter." Parnell grinned. "I sure hope the Doc can keep her alive after using that machine. She and I can have some fun."

Doc Stone's eyes widened, and Parnell turned to him. "You should have guessed why you're here."

"I won't do it," Doc Stone said in a calm, even-toned voice. "You can't make me."

"What if I break every bone in your body?" Parnell asked. "I'll start with your toes."

"You son of a bitch," West growled.

"Ah...see, now you're talking. You just needed the right incentive."

West's lips tilted at the corner, spotting the blood seeping through Parnell's shirt. "Looks like someone got the best of you."

"Damien did," Roni said, fighting her binds. "Should have stabbed him through the heart."

"Judging by the looks of it, he came close," Doc Stone said. "Untie me and let me take a look."

Parnell waved the knife in the air and tisked. "When we're done, I'll be the last patient you ever work on."

"That machine only connects with dead people, and even still, it's useless unless you have something Cree can hold that is emotionally tied to the victim. The people you want dead are still alive. Was all of this going to be worth me killing you?" West asked.

Parnell threw the knife. The sharp silver blade embedded into the seat of West's chair. If he hadn't been fast enough to spread his legs, it would have punctured his leg.

"You'll be long dead before I untie you."

An uncontrollable laugh bubbled deep in West's chest, slipping past his lips.

"You think this is funny?" Parnell asked, stalking to West's chair.

"You underestimate my wife," West said. "It's typical, everybody does." West used the force of his weight to ram his forehead into Parnell's when he reached for the knife.

Parnell stumbled backward.

"If you leave now, they won't kill you."

"They don't even know where you are," Parnell spat.

"You used to be smarter than this. You used to do your research. Do you realize who you've taken? You've got a target on your back that will never go away."

"Some punk teen, a doctor, and you. I think I'll manage even if your wife sends ghosts to keep me awake."

West almost had the knot undone. He only needed a few more minutes to stall. "That teen is engaged to a mob boss's nephew. The doctor is best friends with the everyone on the police force, and me...well, you've met my wife. She's crazy and unpredictable."

Parnell glanced at his watch. "Her time is limited. If I had to guess, Nunnery has already finished her off by now. I'd wager he's about to walk in through that door with condolences."

West

Chapter 19

The door opened, and Cree walked in with a gun pointed at Parnell. She tossed the bloodstained Secret Service badge into the middle of the room. "I'm not sorry for your loss. It looks like your employer had a little accident. He's going to be delayed indefinitely since I have no plans to talk to his dead corpse."

"Shoot this bastard, Cree," Roni yelled.

Cree cocked the trigger and raised her brow just as red laser lights appeared through the window, landing on Parnell's chest and face.

Parnell dropped the knife and held up his hands.

"Why did you want my machine?"

"The bitch is the only one who knows where she hid my stuff."

"What did the prostitute have of yours?" West asked.

"Oh, that's easy, dear," Cree answered. "Proof. She was a witness to all the people he killed from the contracts Nunnery placed. She also stole Parnell's money and hid that and the proof that he was the one who did all the dirty deeds."

Parnell's brows dipped. "How do you know about that?"

"Because she's good. I've been telling you all along, but no one ever listens," West said, pulling his arms free and letting the rope fall behind him. He bent down by Cree's leg and grabbed her knife, exchanging it for the gun she held in her hands. "Cut their ties, luv."

"You underestimated me. Special Agent Hunter was closing in on you. He checked your passport and put you in town when they all died."

"Hunter is a madman. He's not even an agent. You can't trust him."

"He played you. Deputy Director Reed was never looking for the antidote. Why would he when Nunnery only administered the flu? Kind of pathetic if you ask me. It was a ploy to drive you into the open, and it worked."

Cree cut the rope binding Roni and had to hold her back from going after Parnell's throat.

"Tell me, was it was worth your life?" West asked.

"You aren't going to kill me," he said, holding out his arms. "You would have done it by now, and the feds are outside. They'd arrest you for murder."

Cree untied Doc Stone's hands and helped him out of the chair before turning back to Parnell. "Aw, that's sweet. You really are gullible. You think the feds are going to save you? Newsflash, asshole. Those aren't feds." Cree tisked. "They're your worst nightmare."

Moreno walked in, cracking his knuckles, flanked by a few of his intimidating thugs. "We'll take it from here, Cree."

West gestured for Doc Stone and Roni to leave the cabin, and Cree patted Moreno's shoulder. "Now remember what I said."

"Incapacitate, don't kill," Moreno grumbled.

"Right, we need him in one piece delivered to the FBI to make him accountable." Cree glanced back and down at Parnell's crotch. "Well, we don't need all of his pieces."

"I'll have the machine delivered when I'm done."

"No need. I won't be using it anymore."

She'd barely made it out the door when West stopped her and looked her over. "Are you hurt?"

"No, but my new hardwood floors are. Do you think brain matter and blood will be easy to get out?"

He smiled and leaned in to kiss her. "I'll take care of it."

"I knew I married you for a reason."

He winked and tossed his arm over her shoulder, heading to the Jeep where Roni and Doc Stone were already seated.

"It is a normal husbandly thing to do."

Screams came from inside the abandoned farmhouse. One of Moreno's men peered outside. "Sorry. We thought you left."

Cree waved. "We're fine. Keep doing what you're doing. Just remind Moreno what I said."

The man answered with a brief hand gesture before disappearing back inside.

"I need to see Damien," Roni said, leaning forward.

"And I have surgery," Doc Stone said.

West leaned in to kiss her. "We'll chauffeur. Think of it as practice for our kids."

She grinned. "You have all that money. I'm expecting you to hire a driver. Preferably one trained to kill and not one of your old friends."

"I think we can arrange that. I'll see you at home."

DEADLY BLISS

Chapter 20

Two Months Later

West squeezed my hand and lolled his head in my direction. "Mrs. Blue."

"Don't you mean Mrs. Archer?" I smiled, content for the first time in forever. After all that had gone down with Nunnery and Parnell, West had taken me on that honeymoon he'd promised. It seemed coming close to dying also changed him. He now understood my reluctance to help with the murder cases like I had in the past.

I still heard voices in my head. The dead still appeared wanting help. The only difference was I no longer used Insight. Moreno returned the machine, and it now sat idle in the basement covered with one of Grammy's old sheets.

"Keeping my name, then?" he asked, leaning in to kiss me as the plane started its descent into this new town we'd call our temporary home.

"It's growing on me."

"Good to hear," he said, bringing our linked hands up to his mouth and placing a tender kiss.

"Quantico is going to love you."

I didn't believe that for a second. Being in a new town with a new job wasn't something I'd ever thought would happen to me. Growing up I'd hoped it would, but it was only in dreams of venturing to faraway places.

The overhead speaker came on along with the fasten seatbelt warning. "Mr. and Mrs. West. We're second in line to land. It's seventy-two degrees on the ground, and your transportation is waiting."

Butterflies danced in my stomach, and I grinned. This was it. This was my new normal.

As the plane landed and pulled up to the waiting dark SUVs, I couldn't help but feel like a fish out of sea. The lights were so bright in this part of the world.

West nodded at the pilot in passing as we headed down the stairs to be greeted by smiling faces and open arms. Glynis squealed, pulling me into a hug as Deputy Director Reed and Special Agent Hunter stood by.

"This is going to be fabulous," Glynis said, letting me go. "We're going to have so much fun."

"Now I don't remember fun being on the agenda," Harrison said.

"There's always time for crazy good times to make new memories." I wound my arm through Glynis', meeting Harrison's relaxed gaze.

"Office first to meet the other Quantico instructors, and then we'll take you to get settled," Hunter announced.

My smile grew. "I still can't believe you found a place I can fit in."

"What better way to engage their minds than making them practice with cold cases. I think you're going to enjoy teaching," Harrison said.

"Yes, I am," I answered.

"The best and the brightest," Hunter announced. "I'm your liaison and the team leader assigned just to you. Whatever leads you uncover, I'll be following up on."

"Daddy made it happen," Glynis said. "He figured you might have a hard time trusting the other guys to follow through on your leads, but Hunter here will make sure they do."

Never had I thought the FBI would take me seriously. I mean, really, who was I? I Just a small-town girl from the south who talked to the dead and has a penchant for writing warning letters to save people's lives.

I slipped an envelope out of my purse and handed it to Hunter. "I've already got a case picked out."

Hunter peeked inside, and his eyes widened. "This one hasn't even hit the news. How did you know?"

West tossed his arm over my shoulder and kissed the side of my head. "Because she's good and she's my wife."

I smiled up at him. "Remember what you promised."

He leaned into my body. "Don't worry, luv. I've already got a job lined up."

"Really? What's that?" I asked. He hadn't mentioned any job prospects. Not that he needed one.

"I'll be the Mr. Mom while you're at work." He leaned in to whisper in my ear. "Roni told me your Grams and daddy showed up before we left. They wanted us to start stocking up on diapers. Two down, one to go."

"Twins!" God help me.

The End.

DEADLY BLISS

Sign up for her newsletters at www.kateallenton.com

Other Books by Kate Allenton

Suggested Reading Order
BENNETT SISTERS BOX SET (Books 1-4 in one bundle, 1218 pages)
BENNETT SISTERS BOX SET VOLUME 2 (Books 5-7 in one bundle, 517 pages}
INTUITION (Book 1)
TOUCH OF FATE (Book 2)
MIND PLAY (Book 3)
THE RECKONING (Book 4)
REDEMPTION (Book 5)
CHANCE ENCOUNTERS (Book 6)
DESTINED HEARTS (Book 7)

PHANTOM PROTECTORS BOX SET (Books 1-4 in one bundle, 964 pages)
RECKLESS ABANDON (Book 1)
BETRAYAL (Book 2)
UNTAMED (Book 3)
GUIDED LOYALTY (Book 4)

CARRINGTON-HILL INVESTIGATIONS
DECEPTION (Book 1)
DEADLY DESIRE (Book 2)

DEADLY BLISS

DEADLY BLISS

SHIFTER PARADISE BOX SET
NOT MY SHIFTER/ SINFULLY CURSED

KARMA

SOPHIE MASTERSON SERIES/ DIXON SECURITY
LIFTING THE VEIL (Book 1)
BEYOND THE VEIL (Book 2)
VEILED INTENTIONS (Book 3)
VEILED THREATS (Book 4)

THE LOVE FAMILY SERIES
SKYLAR (BOOK1)
DECLAN (BOOK 2)
FLYNN (BOOK 3)
REED (BOOK 4)
LANDON (BOOK 5)
ALEXIS (BOOK 6)
GABE (BOOK 7)
JACKSON (BOOK 8)

LINKED INC.
DEADLY INTENT (BOOK 1)
PSYCHIC LINK (BOOK 2)
PSYCHIC CHARM (BOOK 3)
PSYCHIC GAMES (BOOK 4)
DEADLY DREAMS (BOOK 5)

DEADLY BLISS

CREE BLUE PSYCHIC EYE
DEAD WRONG (BOOK 1)
DEADLY VOWS (BOOK 2)
DEAD FAMOUS (BOOK 3)
DEADLY TIES (BOOK 4)
DEADLY BLISS (BOOK5)

HELL BOUND
MYSTIC TIDES BOX SET
MYSTIC LUCK BOX SET
MAID OF HONOR
HARD SHIFT

DEADLY BLISS

About the Author

Kate has lived in Florida for most of her entire life. She enjoys a quiet life with her husband, Michael and two kids.

Kate has pulled all-nighters finishing her favorite books and also writing them. She says she'll sleep when she's dead or when her muse stops singing off key.

She loves creating worlds full of suspense, secrets, hunky men, kick ass heroines, steamy sex and oh yeah the love of a lifetime. Not to mention an occasional ghost and other supernatural talents thrown into the mix.
Sign up for her newsletters HERE
She loves to hear from her readers by email at KateAllenton@hotmail.com, on Twitter@KateAllenton, and on Facebook at facebook.com/kateallenton.1
Visit her website at www.kateallenton.com
Visit Coastal Escape Publishing's website at www.coastalescapepublishing.com

Made in the USA
Middletown, DE
08 January 2019